PENGUIN CLASSICS

RUDIN

IVAN TURGENEV, Russian novelist, was born in Oryol in 1818, and was the first Russian writer to enjoy an international reputation. Born into the gentry himself, and dominated in his boyhood by a tyrannical mother, he swore a 'Hannibal's oath' against serfdom. After studying in Moscow, St Petersburg, and Berlin (1834–41), where he was influenced by German Idealism, he returned to Russia an ardent liberal and Westernist. He gained fame as an author with a series of brilliant, sensitive pictures of peasant life. Although he had also written poetry, plays and short stories, it was as a novelist that his greatest work was to be done. His novels are noted for the poetic 'atmosphere' of their country settings, the contrast between hero and heroine, and for the objective portrayal of heroes representative of stages in the development of the Russian intelligentsia during the period 1840–70. Exiled to his estate of Spasskoye in 1852 for an obituary of Gogol, he wrote *Rudin* (1856), *Home of the Gentry* (1859), *On the Eve* (1860), *Fathers and Children* (1862), but was so disillusioned by the obtuse criticism which greeted this last work that he spent most of the rest of his life at Baden-Baden (1862–70), and Paris (1871–83). His last novels *Smoke* (1867), and *Virgin Soil* (1877), lacked the balance and topicality of his earlier work. He died in Bougival, near Paris, in 1883.

•

RICHARD FREEBORN is at present Professor of Russian Literature at the School of Slavonic and East European Studies, University of London. He was previously Professor of Russian at Manchester University, a visiting Professor at the University of California at Los Angeles, and for ten years he was Hulme Lecturer in Russian at Brasenose College, Oxford, where he graduated. His publications include *Turgenev, A Study* (1960), *A Short History of Modern Russia* (1966; 1967), a translation of *Sketches from a Hunter's Album* (Penguin Classics, 1967), *The Russian Revolutionary Novel: Turgenev to Pasternak* and a couple of novels.

Ivan Turgenev

RUDIN

TRANSLATED BY
RICHARD FREEBORN

Penguin Books

Penguin Books Ltd, Harmondsworth, Middlesex, England
Viking Penguin Inc., 40 West 23rd Street, New York, New York 10010, U.S.A.
Penguin Books Australia Ltd, Ringwood, Victoria, Australia
Penguin Books Canada Limited, 2801 John Street, Markham, Ontario, Canada L3R 1B4
Penguin Books (N.Z.) Ltd, 182–190 Wairau Road, Auckland 10, New Zealand

—

This translation first published 1975
Reprinted 1976, 1979, 1981, 1983, 1986

—

—

Printed and bound in Great Britain by
Cox & Wyman Ltd, Reading

To Tim and Lal

Introduction

The Tsar of all the Russias, he is strong, with so many bayonets, Cossacks and cannons; and he does a great feat in keeping such a tract of Earth politically together; but he cannot yet speak. Something great in him, but it is a dumb greatness. He has had no voice of genius, to be heard of all men and all times. He must learn to speak. He is a great dumb monster hitherto. His cannons and Cossacks will all have rusted into nonentity, while that Dante's voice is still audible. The Nation that has a Dante is bound together as no dumb Russia can be.

CARLYLE spoke these words in 1840; Turgenev probably first came across them in 1855 when he was contemplating the idea for his first novel, *Rudin*. That year was decisive for imperial Russia. The Tsar of all the Russias to whom Carlyle refers, Emperor Nicholas I, had died at the moment when his military power was being challenged by the allied armies of Great Britain, France, and Turkey besieging Sebastopol. By the summer of that year, at the height of the Crimean War, defeat was imminent. A time of reckoning had arrived. Past assumptions of imperial Russia's role as the gendarme of Europe and her impregnability as a bastion of political autocracy were being abandoned. Talk of reform was in the air. The Russian government, under Alexander II, was beginning to experience that crisis of confidence which was to lead to the implementation of many internal reforms, chief among them being the emancipation of the serfs in 1861. Simultaneously, the Russian nobility, until that time the only educated stratum in Russian society, found itself challenged by a radical-minded younger generation who, in social terms, owed nothing to the established system and, in ideological terms, was ready to repudiate all authority in the name of a revolutionary future. This meant that the intelligentsia of the nobility, to whom Turgenev and the older generation belonged, was confronted by a radical intelligentsia who had no vested interest in serfdom, scorned liberalism and some of the most sacred ideas about art and the individual personality which the older generation esteemed so highly.

Russia had no Dante, strictly speaking, it is true, and despite the power of the autocracy it was a country, even in 1840, beset by serious economic and social troubles, but Carlyle was wrong in supposing that Russia had no voice. Russia had learned to speak with the voice of Pushkin, though it was speaking largely to itself. By 1855, eighteen years after Pushkin's death and three years since Gogol's, Russia may still have seemed dumb to the outside world. Even to itself Russia could not speak freely, due to the censorship. The most articulate voice of the first generation of the Russian intelligentsia, Alexander Herzen, had left Russia for voluntary exile in the West, chiefly in London, in 1847, and there, through the publication of his journal the *Bell*, he became the most influential Russian publicist of the 1850s. In Russia itself the most important forum for new ideas was the journal the *Contemporary*, which Pushkin had established in 1836 and to which Turgenev had sent all his most important work, especially the *Sketches* of peasant life that first brought him fame.* By 1855 the editorial policy of the *Contemporary* was becoming influenced by the radical and materialist ideas of a newcomer, N. G. Chernyshevsky. He was to turn the journal, though it was edited by Nekrasov and Panaev who were both of Turgenev's generation, into the most influential radical organ of its day. In doing so he was to alienate Turgenev and many like him. But, sensitive as he always was to the trends of his epoch and generally more prescient than his contemporaries, Turgenev could appreciate in 1855 that the socio-political

* *Sketches from a Hunter's Album*, translated by Richard Freeborn, Penguin Books, 1972.

8

climate was changing, that new voices were beginning to be heard and new ideas were at hand. He was also aware that the time had come to reappraise the role of the intelligentsia in Russian society. As a novelist he was to become both the intelligentsia's chronicler and its critic; he was also to champion its role in Russian life as the principal medium for the dissemination of ideas beneficial to the whole of Russian society and essential to its future welfare. In *Rudin* he was to demonstrate that through the older generation of the intelligentsia Russia was beginning to acquire a voice – the voice of the 'men of the forties', as they were called, of those like Turgenev himself who had reached maturity in the decade when Carlyle described Russia as a great, dumb monster.

It is a commonplace of critical writing on Turgenev's first novel to assume that Rudin is a further, and in some ways a final, development of the type of 'superfluous man' familiar already in his work from such studies as Rakitin in his play *A Month in the Country*, Chulkaturin of *The Diary of a Superfluous Man*, and the anonymous Hamlet of *Hamlet of the Shchigrovsky District*. The superfluity of the 'superfluous man' is to be interpreted chiefly in social terms, as of someone, a man of often real talent, who can find no place for himself in the society of his time. Turgenev attempted both to document and to vindicate the existence of this type in Russian society, emphasizing the 'superfluous man's' tragic condition and his comic inadequacies. There is little doubt that the frailties which we can so easily discern in Rudin are present in the earlier studies – the division of head and heart, the undue intellectualizing of life's problems, the introspectiveness and indecisiveness so characteristic of the Hamlet type, the self-mistrust which evolves so quickly into masochistic self-humiliation, and an exhibitionist need to confess. But Rudin, though he evinces such weaknesses as much as any 'superfluous man', is deliberately portrayed by Turgenev as more than the sum of these weaknesses. He may be a failure in a practical sense, but he differs from preceding studies in that certain heroic features are carefully incorporated in his character which clearly emphasize his social relevance.

Ever since the early 1850s Turgenev had been toying with the idea of a large novel to be called *Two Generations*. By 1855 this project had got little further than its preliminary stages, and he appears to have abandoned it in order to write what we now know as his first novel. The idea for *Rudin* came to him in June 1855, possibly while three close friends of his, Botkin, Grigorovich, and Druzhinin, were staying with him at his country estate of Spasskoye, or perhaps shortly after their departure. Much of the three weeks his friends spent with him was taken up with amateur theatricals. A play called *The School for Hospitality* was produced and most successfully performed. It had none of the pre-Chekhovian manner of his only full-length play, *A Month in the Country* (1850), which was banned by the censors and not given a public performance until more than twenty years after it was written, but at least it must have had the effect of making Turgenev think about problems of theatrical presentation and, above all, dialogue. From this experience, one suspects, came the noticeably theatrical form of *Rudin* – much of the novel reads like a play, especially in the scenes between Lezhnev, Volyntsev and Alexandra Lipin – and the emphasis upon scene-by-scene presentation of the events.

A more important influence of his friends' visit to Spasskoye may have been the interest at that time of V. P. Botkin in the work of Thomas Carlyle. Botkin was one of Turgenev's literary advisers; it was he who urged Turgenev to write *Rudin*, judging at least from Turgenev's letter to him of 17 June 1855. No doubt Botkin also showed him the passage from Carlyle quoted at the beginning of this Introduction, in which Russia is declared to have had 'no voice of genius' (this passage, incidentally, did not appear in the translation which Botkin published in the *Contemporary* at the beginning of

1856, in the same issue as the first part of *Rudin*). We can assume that Turgenev and Botkin must have discussed some of the ideas raised by Carlyle in his *Heroes and Hero-Worship* and that they may have acted upon Turgenev as a catalyst in directing his attention towards a type of character like Rudin.

Carlyle acknowledged that it was common for contemporary critics to deride the worship of great men: 'Show our critics a great man ... they begin to what they call "account" for him; not to worship him, but take the dimensions of him – and bring him out to be a little kind of man!' Such a process is clearly observable in Turgenev's portrayal of Rudin. But Carlyle sought to reinstate the heroic ideal in the public mind and for that purpose he tried to define the qualities which contributed to a man's heroic proportions. Foremost among these was what a man believed, or as Carlyle put it: '... the thing a man does practically believe ... the thing a man does practically lay to heart, and know for certain, concerning his vital relations to this mysterious Universe, and his duty and destiny there, that is in all cases the primary thing for him, and creatively determines all the rest. That is his *religion* ...' Turgenev would have understood this at once: it was no church religion, of course, but the sum of a man's noblest convictions as a human being. Rudin asserts the vital importance for a man of having such convictions at his first appearance in the novel, so that he is able to oppose and outface the scepticism of the local wiseacre Pigasov. Rudin is acclaimed at the start for his eloquence in articulating his beliefs. He never loses this eloquence, though it may begin to sound, as the novel progresses, increasingly like so much phrase-mongering. Such eloquence is precisely what Carlyle commends as a mark of the hero, for, in being able to discern and express the loveliness of things, men call such a hero 'Poet, Painter, Man of Genius, gifted, lovable'; and Carlyle traces this kind of hero back to the Norse Odin and his Runes (it would be a nice conceit to think that Runes+Odin = Rudin) who first 'invented

Poetry; the music of human speech, as well as that miraculous runic marking of it'. Rudin is similarly commended for the poetry of his eloquence when he concludes his first triumphal evening with a 'Scandinavian' legend[*] – Darya Lasunsky admits as much: '*Vous êtes un poète*' – and we are told that Rudin possessed 'what is almost the highest secret – the music of eloquence'. In other words, Turgenev has endowed his hero with some of those heroic qualities which Carlyle attempted to define, even if it may be far-fetched to adduce any specific relationship between Carlyle's text and Turgenev's portrayal. Turgenev did not meet Carlyle personally until 1857. He was never naturally given to the veneration of heroes as was the Chelsea Sage, but it is clear that he sought to endow Rudin with more 'heroic' qualities than he had given to his previous studies of 'superfluous men'.

It is equally clear that he intended the portrait to be critical. In his letter of 17 June to Botkin, he insisted: 'There are epochs when literature cannot be *only* art – but there are interests higher than poetic interests, a moment of self-awareness and criticism is as essential in the development of a nation's life as it is in the life of an individual person . . .' The portrait of Rudin was critical in the sense that it would make or break his own reputation as a writer. If the portrait failed, he planned to abandon writing for good; but he was given to this kind of periodic despair. The portrait was also critical in the sense that it was partly an act of self-scrutiny, undertaken during June and July 1855 when an outbreak of cholera forced him to remain at Spasskoye rather than go grouse-shooting as he had hoped. In this time he rapidly wrote the first draft of his novel. But of course it was also an act of criticism directed against the Russian intelligentsia of his own

[*] Commentators have pointed out that the legend of the little bird which flies into the lighted hall and then out into the darkness again is apparently not to be found in Scandinavian folklore but comes from the Venerable Bede (see Chapter III, note 1).

generation. Through critical scrutiny of his own generation's inadequacies he was attempting to define the true role of the Russian intelligentsia in the future. At this very moment, however, he first encountered the materialist ideas of the radical publicist Chernyshevsky as they were expressed in his dissertation on aesthetics, *The Aesthetic Relations of Art to Reality*. He makes all kind of rude remarks about Chernyshevsky in his letters at this time, until he clarifies his antagonism in a letter of 25 July to Botkin and Nekrasov: 'So far as Chernyshevsky's book is concerned, here's my principal charge against it: in his eyes art is, as he puts it, only a surrogate of reality and life – and it is only good in fact for immature people. No matter how you look at it, this idea lies at the base of everything he says. But in my opinion this is nonsense. In reality there is no such person as Shakespeare's Hamlet – or maybe there is, and Shakespeare discovered him, and made him accessible to all.' Obviously what hurt him in Chernyshevsky's attitude was the presumption that art was merely a kind of appendix to life and that the writer could never create anything new, let alone produce such a universal image of man as had Shakespeare in Hamlet. This view of art would be likely to misinterpret, if not wholly misunderstand, a relatively sophisticated type – a mixture of Hamlet and Don Quixote, of eloquent intellect and cold heart – such as he had created in Rudin.

There were grounds, then, for his apprehensions about the central portrait. It was intended to be a critical examination of a type of intellectual common to Turgenev's own generation of the Russian intelligentsia. But it was also modelled, as Turgenev was ready to admit, on certain specific individuals, chiefly his former friend and intellectual guide, Mikhail Bakunin. Bakunin had always possessed eloquence allied to philosophical interests, even if these interests may have changed from the German idealism which so attracted him when Turgenev had known him as a student in Berlin in the early

1840s to an interest in anarchism by the 1850s. Turgenev drew on other traits of his former friend – his propensity for domineering over others, interfering in their private affairs, borrowing their money, and perhaps also his impotence – in painting the portrait of Rudin. The draft of the novel which Turgenev took with him when he left Spasskoye for Moscow in October contained all these elements. He arrived in Moscow in time to attend the funeral of one of the most beloved and revered members of his own generation, Professor Granovsky. In his obituary notice, written on the day after the funeral, he made the following warm tribute:

Devoid of pedantry, full of an engaging kindliness, he even then* could arouse that spontaneous respect which so many were to experience later. He emanated a kind of exaltedly pure influence; it was given to him (a rare and blessed gift) to awaken a sense of the beautiful in another's soul not through expression of his convictions, not by argument, but by his own spiritual beauty; he was an idealist in the best sense of this word, in the sense that he was not an idealist in isolation. He had a perfect right to say: *Humani nihil a me alienum puto*, and therefore nothing human felt alien to him.

A few years later I met him in Berlin. I saw almost nothing of him then – and we did not get on ... To tell the truth, I didn't deserve to get on with him then. Besides, at that time he had made friends with N. V. Stankevich, a man about whom it's impossible to say little, but about whom this is not the time and place to say much. Stankevich had a very great influence on Granovsky, and part of his spirit entered into him.

The death of Granovsky obliged Turgenev to reconsider his portrait of Rudin. We may suppose that he was as determined as ever to emphasize the idealism and love of beauty which Rudin professed, if only in opposition to the materialism and utilitarianism of Chernyshevsky's views, but he must have been equally concerned both to disguise any undue resemblance to Bakunin in the portrait and to illustrate how

*When Turgenev knew him at the University of St Petersburg.

14

altruistic and idealistic had been the ideas which animated his own generation in its youth. It had become imperative to disguise to some extent the resemblance to Bakunin because in the autumn of 1855 Bakunin had been handed over to the Russian authorities by the Austrian government and imprisoned. In view of this, those to whom Turgenev read the draft of his novel when he reached St Petersburg apparently felt the need for certain changes. Rudin's portrait was to be enlarged and deepened, in part at least to diminish, although not to obscure, the pettinesses in his character, and Turgenev therefore introduced in what is now Chapter VI of the novel the lengthy description by Lezhnev of his student experiences with Rudin in the Pokorsky circle. The contrast made between Rudin and Pokorsky has been considered by many commentators to reflect Turgenev's view of the differences between Bakunin and Stankevich, between the youthful Demosthenes whose eloquence could range over a whole spectrum of received opinion and the original genius who, though less superficially spectacular, had the power to stir noble feelings in the most bestial of men 'just as if you'd unstoppered a forgotten scent bottle in a dark and dirty room'.

The other major change was the addition of the epilogue in which Lezhnev meets Rudin for the last time and modifies his former harsh judgements. Four years after the novel was first published – in 1860 – Turgenev added the final scene describing Rudin's death on the Paris barricades of 1848. This scene, so specific in its historical reference, has the effect of distorting the chronology of the novel as a whole. We have to assume that Turgenev intended the main action of the novel to occur at some point in the mid 1840s, with the first meeting between Rudin and Lezhnev occurring approximately in the middle of the previous decade (in other words, during Turgenev's own university years), so that by the opening of the novel Rudin and Lezhnev would be respectively 35 and 30 years of age. They can be said, therefore, to belong to the 'men of the forties'. On the first publication of the novel in the *Contemporary* in 1856 it was divided into two parts, but this division was not made in any later editions. In the first French translation of the novel, done by Turgenev himself in collaboration with Louis Viardot, Pauline Viardot's husband, and published in 1862, the chapters were renumbered and some minor changes were made in the text, among the most interesting being the amplification of Lezhnev's censure of Rudin's lack of *'natura'* (in the Russian) into *'Ce qui lui manque, c'est la volonté, c'est le nerf, la force.'** Otherwise, apart from minor corrections, the text of the novel remained as in its 1860 form throughout Turgenev's lifetime, even to the extent of retaining Natalya's apparent uncertainty about Rudin's patronymic: normally she addresses him as Dmitry Nikolaich, but at moments of stress (as in Chapter VII) he becomes Dmitry Nikolayevich.

The reworkings and additions which the novel underwent obviously tended to blur some of the detail of the central portrait, but however blurred or slightly faded at the edges it may be, with perhaps a little of that discoloration which age lends to old photographs, it still has clear, vital features. Turgenev has succeeded in catching a living resemblance, and the secret of that vitality is to be sought in the inherent interest of the man himself. As Lord David Cecil put it in his introduction to an earlier and very fine translation of this novel by Alec Brown (1950), Turgenev's

picture of humanity is conscientiously true to the facts: but the facts he chooses to portray are interesting facts. His heroes and heroines are

---

*In this translation the word 'manliness' has been used to express the Russian, on the grounds that the French translation reinforces this idea. For a detailed discussion of the history of the novel's composition, based largely on the elaborate commentary in the Soviet Academy of Sciences edition of Turgenev's works, Vol. VI, Moscow-Leningrad, 1963, see Patrick Waddington's commentary to his edition of *Rudin*, Bradda Books, 1970.

civilized persons of fine nature and deep feelings and questioning minds and delicate charm. Once again he is able, merely by describing them truthfully, to produce something delightful. Why, it has been asked, should one waste hours of one's valuable time in reading about people who, in actual life, one would take pains to avoid? No one ever asks this question after reading a story by Turgenev.

One might, knowing as we do how insufferable he can be, try to avoid people like Rudin in real life. Equally, though, we might receive from him that insight into the truth of life, that glimpse of an ideal or a purpose, which could irradiate like a lightning flash the mundanity of existence and give solace for a lifetime.

Turgenev always liked to claim that he saw his characters like images born in the mind's eye. In one reminiscence he is reported to have said:

Most of all I am pursued by an image, and it takes a long time to grasp hold of it. And the strange thing is that I often get a clear picture first of all of a secondary character, and only later of the main character. For instance, in *Rudin* I first of all had a clear picture of Pigasov, pictured how he began an argument with Rudin, how Rudin repulsed him, and only after that did the portrait of Rudin grow up before my eyes.

There is a ring of truth to this admission. The contrast between the believer and the sceptic, between the genuine enthusiast for ideas and the sarcastic but embittered cynic, is one of great potency. It could so easily become the germinal idea for a novel conceived in rather theatrical terms as a vehicle for a piece of rather unflattering characterization. As we now know it, the effectiveness of the novel and the central portrait is dependent on the establishment of a setting, a fictional place, into which the hero comes as a stranger from the greater outside world and to which he offers a contrast in ideas and attitudes that attracts the heroine, Natalya, through whom in turn, as the relationship develops, we discover the hero's weaknesses. The setting is splendidly achieved, both through the opening description of Alexandra Lipin's visit to the sick peasant woman and through the picture we have of Darya Lasunsky's country mansion. The populace of this little world – Alexandra Pavlovna, Lezhnev, Pandalevsky, Volyntsev, Basistov, Mlle Boncourt, Pigasov, finally Darya Lasunsky herself and her daughter Natalya – springs beautifully to life in conformity to the setting, animated like characters on a stage, accustomed to its ways but unstagily masters and mistresses of their respective roles. The 'nice' people are interestingly nice: Alexandra Lipin, her brother Volyntsev, her admirer Lezhnev, and they have the fairly unaffected, unimaginative, decent niceness of any country squirearchy. They would not be hard to imagine in an English setting. Darya Lasunsky, that overbearing *grande dame*, might appear more exotic, though by no means a contrived character, whereas her sycophantic amanuensis Pandalevsky is a masterly observed piece of sarcastic portraiture. Pigasov, the embittered and witty misogynist, is a genuinely entertaining character who might indeed acquire a reputation as a 'character' in such a limited, snobbish, provincial world. The fictional place and the characters who inhabit it are, quite simply, recognizable, real; but the hero who comes from outside surpasses their limited reality: he lives in the mind after they have vanished into their respective niches in the fiction.

Rudin is tall, personable, plausible, eloquent, and inspiring. We may note that his clothes are not new and look a little tight, that his hands are large and red, but his eyes are splendid, and how the man can talk! He is the idealist who, though they must necessarily be vague and addressed to the future, can make his ideals seem spellbinding and worth a lifetime's sacrifice to accomplish. As Lezhnev put it in final vindication: 'He has enthusiasm; and that, believe me – for I speak as a phlegmatic man – is a most precious quality in our time. We have all become intolerably rational, indifferent and effete; we have gone to sleep, we have grown cold, and we should be grateful to anyone who rouses us and warms us, if only for a moment!' Rudin certainly rouses the company assembled at Darya Lasunsky's house on that early summer evening. Quickly, even if a trifle naïvely, turning the tables on Pigasov by demonstrating the importance of believing in ideas, Rudin goes on to emphasize the need for mankind to have faith in science and knowledge because men must have faith in themselves and their own powers. If a man has no firm principles, he argues, how can he know the needs, the significance, and the future of his people? The question raises the whole matter of the Russian intelligentsia's duty to devote themselves to the future welfare of their country, a task which demands subordination of the ego to some higher cause, as Rudin eloquently claims. His message has a religious appeal, in that he speaks as the high-priest of a religion of service to humanity, to one's country, and the liberation of one's people, and he can clearly stir his listeners' hearts with his ideas. Rudin is no charlatan. But he acknowledges, in the Scandinavian legend which concludes the triumph of his first evening at Darya Lasunsky's, that all human endeavour is ephemeral, that man is fated to no more than the fleeting and insignificant life of a bird's flight out of darkness into light and back to darkness again, and that he, Rudin, is as fated as the next man.

After this triumph the rest is so much failure. Turgenev lightly draws attention to some of his quirks: his habit of appearing surprised by any question related to his past or his role in life, and his tendency to repeat the question before answering, his relative failure as a storyteller, his lack of humour, his weakness as a conversationalist, despite his capacity for being a good listener. In his relations with Natalya we see how his words are challenged, how she, in her disarming candour and formidable innocence, can see the lack of purpose but still be fascinated by the man's erudition, particularly his knowledge of German literature and thought. When he admits that he has so far been unable to clarify for himself the tragic significance of love, it is clear that he is no more than the analyst, the clever, eloquent intellectual, who can pose as one possessing an understanding of the ways of the heart without really knowing how that pose can be misinterpreted by his impressionable audience. The revelation that she loves him induces in him a form of crisis of identity: does he really love her, is he really happy, did he deliberately turn the poor girl's head? Rudin lacks the fresh, emotional spontaneity which could allow him to respond to Natalya's love. We may also presume that this talk perhaps hides an impotence of both sexuality and character that foredooms him. When, meeting for that last time, in the sombre environs of the Avdyukhin pond, Natalya expects him to act, all he can do is utter the word: 'Submit' – submit, that is, to his own weakness of will, his poverty, Darya Lasunsky's displeasure, to fate, to the impossibility of happiness, that special idea at the heart of Turgenev's pessimism. By this time Rudin has been stripped of all his former grandeur. All he can lay claim to when he leaves Darya Lasunsky's house, speaking to his most ardent disciple Basistov, is his advocacy of freedom in the manner of a Don Quixote. Little enough though it may seem, that advocacy is to redeem him for all his faults.

Of course Rudin is no Great Man, as Carlyle would have it. His pettinesses clamour for recognition just as he spitefully cries out to Natalya when she leaves him at the Avdyukhin pond: '*You* are the coward, not me!' For her part, Natalya appears to be seeking in Rudin a father-figure rather than a lover. We have to take Turgenev's word for it that she is deep. Superficially she seems intense, humourless, serious, almost dull, but we can easily accept that her innocent nature needs the experience and maturity of Rudin in order to fulfil it. She needs the seriousness which the frivolous sophistication of her mother cannot give her. The tragedy of the relationship lies as much in her emotional need as in Rudin's weakness. As I have expressed it elsewhere: 'The mutual need of hero and heroine must be understood as one of self-fulfilment, self-completion, supposedly to be attained in the happiness of a requited love, though in fact – as all Turgenev's studies ultimately reveal – such fulfilment is an impossibility, the love is always guilty and, in part, illicit.'* Natalya's was a nature emotionally vulnerable to the influence of a Rudin and hers is also the destiny to endure the torments of first love, though, as Turgenev reminds us in this novel and in so many other studies, 'first sufferings, like first love, are not repeated – thank God!'

To Volyntsev, Rudin's behaviour in seeking his assent to Natalya's love seems outrageous. Rudin's reference, what is more, to the hope that Volyntsev might rise above his surroundings neatly points out the limitations of the provincial squirearchy, however apparently decent they may seem. Rudin's advocacy of a franker, more magnanimous attitude to human relations may appear preposterous to his stuffy, gentlemanly rival, but the idealism of it ultimately reveals his fundamental superiority. The lack of 'manliness' and the cosmopolitanism of which Lezhnev accuses him are compensated for by the many good seeds which he has sown in young hearts. At their final meeting all Lezhnev's former censure dissolves into an excessively emotional rehabilitation of the hapless hero. Rudin's account of his failures is as comic as it is tragic. By any standards he is to be regarded as one of life's losers, though by the standards of a capitalist society he is to be accounted a failure. Rudin nevertheless insists that in none of his enterprises or ideas has he ever been other than loyal. He may have sought to encourage new ideas, as Basistov enthusiastically claimed, 'he could make you get up and go, he never let you grow settled in your ways, he

*Richard Freeborn, *Turgenev, The Novelist's Novelist*, OUP, 1960, p. 113.

turned the very foundation of things upside down, he set light to you!' but he never aspired actively, so far as one can tell, to promote revolution. The 'revolutionizing' of Rudin which occurs with the final scene depicting his death is not gratuitous; it seems to fit the preceding portrayal in the sense that one can well imagine how Rudin might wish to end his life with a bold, theatrical gesture. For Turgenev it may have meant something different. He added the scene in 1860, perhaps when he was contemplating the actual revolutionary role of the Russian intelligentsia in the form of his most obviously 're-formist' hero, Bazarov of *Fathers and Children*, and in making Rudin end as a revolutionary he was tacitly acknowledging the revolutionary aspiration of the Fathers, those, in other words, of his own generation. Save that Turgenev, unlike Herzen or Ogaryov, never 'fell at someone's feet' as does his hero in the service of a revolutionary cause.

The novel is neatly composed, its atmosphere evoked by Turgenev's gift for nature description, and each character, however minor, comes sharply into focus whether simply through the dialogue, or by a description of external appearances, or the introduction of biographical material. Turgenev's wit enlivens and tautens the portraiture – how wickedly well-judged, for example, is the portrayal of Darya Lasunsky – and can score off pomposity with a deftly crushing description, like that of the young Korchagin who 'used to adopt unusually majestic poses, as if he were not a living person at all, but his own statue erected by public subscription.' When he is being indulgent, as he is on occasion, one feels, with Lezhnev and Volyntsev, he perhaps makes claims for them which overrate their inherent interest as characters. As for the love story, it has charm and a certain poignancy; it is also the most old-fashioned feature of the novel. The sceptic may be forgiven for feeling relief at Rudin's apparently craven readiness to submit to fate once the relationship with Natalya has been discovered. On his part, so the sceptic may feel, it at least has the merit of common sense, no matter how far it may fall short of the strong-minded Natalya's ideas. They were not an ideally suited pair and it would be wishful thinking to suppose that such disparate personalities could ever make common cause for a lifetime.

The novel aroused keen controversy and interest when it first appeared. The image of Rudin, the failure redeemed by his enthusiasm and idealism, entered the Russian national consciousness almost as deeply as did Gonacharov's Oblomov. But Rudin is not so 'national' a figure; he has so many characteristics that could belong as readily to intellectuals in any fairly civilized setting as to the Russian intelligentsia. Many stressed his cosmopolitanism, his germanophile characteristics. According to Dostoyevsky, whose hatred of Turgenev's germanophile sympathies is well known, the novel simply could not be understood by non-Russian readers. 'Translate Turgenev's novel *Rudin*', he thundered, '(I mention Turgenev because he has been translated more than other Russian authors, and the novel *Rudin*, because of all Turgenev's works it most resembles something German) into any European language and even then it will not be understood.' Perhaps the novel will not be understood – this is a significant part of its interest as a portrayal of failure – but this translation, by trying to render the original as faithfully as possible, even to the extent of reproducing much of Turgenev's punctuation, has endeavoured to do no more than make the Russian text easily comprehensible, so that readers can decide for themselves whether or not they understand the portrait of Rudin.

RUDIN

Characters in alphabetical order of first name

Since *Rudin* reads in parts so much like a play, and because the characters are so often referred to by name and patronymic (i.e. their father's name), a guide to their formal names, as well as the familiar forms of address, may be helpful.

Afrikan Semyonych Pigasov

Alexandra Pavlovna Lipin (*fam.* Sasha, *sister of Volyntsev*)

Darya Mikhaylovna Lasunsky (*mother of Natalya*)

Dmitry Nikolaich (Nikolayevich) Rudin (*fam.* Mitya)

Konstantin Diomidych Pandalevsky

Mikhaylo Mikhaylych Lezhnev (*fam.* Misha)

Natalya Alexeyevna Lasunsky (*daughter of Darya Lasunsky*)

Sergey Pavlych Volyntsev (*fam.* Seryozha, *brother of Alexandra Lipin*)

I

IT was a quiet summer morning. The sun was already fairly high in a clear sky; but the fields still glistened with dew, from newly awakened hollows rose a fragrant freshness and in woodland, still damp and unrustling, there could be heard the gay sound of early birdsong. On the summit of a gentle hill, covered from top to bottom with newly blossomed rye, a small village could be seen. Towards this little village, along a narrow cross-country track, a young woman walked, in a white muslin dress and round straw hat, carrying a parasol. A servant-boy followed some distance behind her.

She walked without hurrying, seeming to enjoy her stroll. All around her through the high swaying rye, criss-crossing first in silvery-green, then in reddish ripples, ran long waves accompanied by a soft rustling; in the sky the larks pealed out their song. The young woman was walking from her own village, no more than two thirds of a mile from the little village to which she was making her way; she was Alexandra Pavlovna Lipin. She was a widow, childless and fairly wealthy, and she lived with her brother, a retired staff-captain, Sergey Pavlych Volyntsev. He was unmarried and looked after her estate.

Alexandra Pavlovna reached the little village, stopped at the outermost, extremely ancient and low-pitched hut, and, summoning her servant-boy, ordered him to go in and ask after the health of the woman who lived there. He quickly came back accompanied by a decrepit peasant with a white beard.

'Well, how is she?' asked Alexandra Pavlovna.

'She's still breathin'...' said the old man.

'May I go in?'

'Why not? 'Course you may.'

Alexandra Pavlovna entered the hut. Inside it was cramped

and stuffy and smoky. Someone began to stir and groan on the stove-bench. Alexandra Pavlovna looked round and saw in the half-light an old woman's yellow, wrinkled head tied with a check handkerchief. Covered right up to her neck with a heavy peasant coat, she was breathing with difficulty, weakly moving her frail hands.

Alexandra Pavlovna approached the old woman and felt her brow. It was literally on fire.

'How do you feel, Matryona?' she asked, bending over the bench.

'O-oh!' groaned the old woman, peering up at Alexandra Pavlovna. 'Poorly, poorly, my dear! The hour of death is come, dear lady!'

'God is merciful, Matryona: you may well get better. Did you take the medicine I sent you?'

The old woman groaned in anguish and did not reply. She had not grasped the question.

'She took it,' said the old man, who had stopped by the door.

Alexandra Pavlovna turned to him.

'Apart from you is there no one looking after her?'

'There's a girl, her granddaughter, 'cept she's away all the time. Won't keep still: right fidgety she is. It's too much for her just to give her gran a drink o' water. An' I'm old; what can I do?'

'Why not have her transferred to my hospital?'

'No! She's for no hospital! She'll die all the same. She's lived a fair while, seein' it's as God would have it. She won't get down from that bench. Where's the point of 'er goin' to hospital? Soon as try liftin' her she'll die.'

'O-oh,' the sick woman started groaning, 'dear, fine lady that you are, don't abandon my little orphan girl; our master's far away, but you . . .'

The old woman fell silent. Speaking had been too much for her.

'Don't worry,' said Alexandra Pavlovna, 'everything will be done. I've brought you some tea and sugar. If you'd like, have a drink ... You've got a samovar, haven't you?' she added, glancing at the old man.

'A samovar? We've got no samovar, but we could get one.'

'Then get one, or I'll send you mine. And tell your grand-daughter not to be away all the time. Tell her she ought to be ashamed.'

The old man did not reply, but took the packet with the tea and sugar in both hands.

'Well, good-bye, Matryona!' said Alexandra Pavlovna. 'I'll come again, and don't lose heart, and be sure to take your medicine regularly ...'

The old woman raised her head and stretched out towards Alexandra Pavlovna.

'Give me your hand, milady,' she babbled.

Alexandra Pavlovna did not offer her hand but bent and kissed her on the brow.

'Make sure,' she said to the old man as she went out, 'that you give her the medicine exactly as prescribed ... And let her have some tea to drink ...'

The old man again made no reply and simply bowed.

Once again Alexandra Pavlovna breathed freely out in the fresh air. She opened her parasol and was about to go home when suddenly round the corner of the hut in a low racing droshky came a man of about thirty wearing an old coat made of grey homespun and a cap of the same material. Seeing Alexandra Pavlovna, he immediately stopped the horse and turned to her. His broad face, without any colouring, with small pale-grey eyes and a whitish moustache, resembled the colour of his clothes.

'How do you do?' he asked with a lazy grin. 'What are you doing here, may I inquire?'

'I have been visiting a sick woman ... And where are you from, Mikhaylo Mikhaylych?'

The man called Mikhaylo Mikhaylych looked her in the eyes and again grinned.

'It's a good thing you're doing,' he continued, 'visiting the sick; only wouldn't it be better for you to transfer her to hospital?'

'She's too weak: she can't be moved.'

'Are you intending to close down your hospital?'

'Close it down? Why?'

'I just thought so.'

'What a strange idea! Whatever put that thought in your head?'

'Well, you never keep anything from Mme Lasunsky and you're apparently under her influence. And in her words hospitals and schools are all a lot of nonsense, so many unnecessary inventions. Charity ought to be personal, education as well: it's all a matter of the spirit ... That's how she expresses herself, it seems. What's she sing that tune for, I'd like to know.'

Alexandra Pavlovna laughed.

'Darya Mikhaylovna is a clever woman, I'm very fond of her and I respect her; but even she can be mistaken, and I don't believe every word she says.'

'And very right, too,' responded Mikhaylo Mikhaylych, remaining seated in the droshky, 'because she herself hardly believes her own words. But I'm very pleased I met you.'

'And what does that mean?'

'A good question! As if it isn't always a pleasure to meet you! Today you're as fresh and charming as this beautiful morning.'

Alexandra Pavlovna again laughed.

'Why do you laugh?'

'Why? If only you could have seen the cold, hang-dog look on your face when you uttered your compliment! I'm surprised you didn't yawn at the end of it!'

'A cold look indeed ... You want fire all the time; but

fire isn't good for anything. It flames, smokes, and goes out.'

'And warms,' added Alexandra Pavlovna.

'Yes – and it can burn you.'

'Well, what if it does burn you! There's no harm in that. It's still better than . . .'

'I'll wait and see if you say the same thing when you *have* really burnt yourself,' Mikhaylo Mikhaylych broke in angrily and struck the horse with the reins. 'Good-bye!'

'Mikhaylo Mikhaylych, stop!' shouted Alexandra Pavlovna. 'When will you be coming to see us?'

'Tomorrow. My regards to your brother.'

And the droshky drove away.

Alexandra Pavlovna gazed after Mikhaylo Mikhaylych.

'What a sack of a man!' she thought. Hunched and dusty, with his cap pulled back on his head so that tufts of yellow hair stuck out beyond it, he did indeed look like a large sack of flour.

Alexandra Pavlovna went calmly back along the track towards home. She walked with downcast eyes. The clatter of horse's hooves close by forced her to stop and raise her head . . . Her brother was riding towards her on horseback; beside him walked a young man of small build in an unbuttoned summery frock-coat, a summery necktie, and a summery grey hat, with a walking-stick in his hand. He had already been smiling for some while in Alexandra Pavlovna's direction, even though he could see that she was walking deep in thought without noticing anything, but as soon as she stopped he went up to her and declared delightedly, almost tenderly:

'How do you do, Alexandra Pavlovna, how do you do!'

'Ah! Konstantin Diomidych! Good morning!' she answered. 'You're coming from Darya Mikhaylovna?'

'Precisely, ma'am, precisely,' the young man agreed with a radiant face. 'I'm from Darya Mikhaylovna. Darya Mikhaylovna has sent me to you, ma'am: I preferred to walk . . . The morning's so delightful and it's only four miles. I reach your home and find you've left. Your dear brother tells me that you've gone to Semyonovka and he is just preparing to ride out himself. So I came with him, ma'am, to meet you. Yes, that's how it was. Isn't it nice!'

The young man spoke Russian clearly and correctly but with a foreign accent, although it was difficult to say exactly what accent it was. There was something Asian about his features. The long hooked nose, the large protuberant motionless eyes, large red lips, receding forehead, hair black as tar – everything about him declared his eastern origins; but the young man had the surname Pandalevsky and called Odessa his birthplace, although he had been brought up somewhere in Belorussia by a wealthy, philanthropic widow. Another widow had found a place for him in the civil service. In general, middle-aged ladies gladly took Konstantin Diomidych under their wing; he had a way of seeking them out and finding his nest among them. Now he was living at the house of the rich estate-owner, Darya Mikhaylovna Lasunsky, as a protégé or hanger-on. He was very affectionate, solicitous, sensitive, and secretly voluptuous, had a pleasant voice, was a competent pianist, and had a habit, when talking to someone, of literally transfixing that person with his eyes. He dressed very neatly and made his clothes last an extraordinarily long time, his broad chin was always meticulously shaved and there was not a hair out of place on his head.

Alexandra Pavlovna heard his speech to the end and turned to her brother:

'Today is nothing but meetings for me: I've just been talking to Lezhnev.'

'Really! Was he going somewhere?'

'Yes; and just imagine, in a racing droshky, dressed in some kind of linen sack, covered in dust ... What an extraordinary man he is!'

'Yes, perhaps; he's a really good sort.'

'Who is? Mr Lezhnev?' asked Pandalevsky, seeming surprised.

'Yes, Mikhaylo Mikhaylych Lezhnev,' rejoined Volyntsev. 'However, my dear, I must say good-bye: it's time for me to be off into the fields to see how they're sowing your buckwheat. Mr Pandalevsky will accompany you home . . .'

And Volyntsev trotted away on his horse.

'With the greatest pleasure!' exclaimed Konstantin Diomidych and offered Alexandra Pavlovna his arm.

She preferred to give him her own arm and both set off along the path to her estate.

To lead Alexandra Pavlovna by the arm evidently afforded Konstantin Diomidych a great deal of pleasure; he took small, mincing steps, was wreathed in smiles, and his eastern eyes were even filled with moisture, which, it should be said, happened to him not infrequently: it cost Konstantin Diomidych no effort at all to feel emotionally involved, even to shed a tear. And who wouldn't have taken pleasure in leading by the arm a pretty woman who was young and elegant? About Alexandra Pavlovna the whole of — province was unanimously of the opinion that she was charming, and — province was not mistaken. Her straight but slightly upturned little nose was alone sufficient to drive any man out of his mind, not to mention her velvety brown little eyes, her russet-gold hair, the dimples in her round little cheeks, and her other charms. But her best feature was the expression of her pretty face: so trusting, good-natured, and unaffected that it was both touching and appealing. Alexandra Pavlovna had the look and laugh of a child; women considered her a little artless . . . Could one wish for more?

'Darya Mikhaylovna sent you to me, you say?' she asked Pandalevsky.

'Yeth, ma'am, she did,' he answered, pronouncing the letter *s* as *th*, 'her ladyship definitely wishes and ordered that you should be earnestly asked to dine with her today ... Her ladyship' (when he spoke of a third person, especially a lady, he always maintained this grand style) '– her ladyship is expecting a new guest whom she definitely wants you to meet.'

'Who is it?'

'A certain Mueffel, a Baron and Kammerjunker,[1] from St Petersburg. Darya Mikhaylovna recently became acquainted with him at Prince Garin's and praised him very highly as an agreeable and educated young man. The Herr Baron also occupies himself with literature or to put it a better way ... Ah, what a charming butterfly! Allow me to direct your attention ... a better way, with political economy. He has written an article on a very interesting question – and he would like to have Darya Mikhaylovna's judgement on it.'

'Her judgement on political economy?'

'From the point of view of the language, ma'am, Alexandra Pavlovna, from the point of view of the language only. I think you know, ma'am, that Darya Mikhaylovna is an expert in this. Zhukovsky[2] has consulted her, and my benefactor who lives in Odessa, the invaluable old man, Roxolan Mediarovich Ksandryka ... You must surely know the name of the gentleman?'

'Not in the least and I've never heard of it.'

'Never heard of the gentleman? Astonishing! I wanted to say that Roxolan Mediarovich also had a very high opinion of Darya Mikhaylovna's knowledge of the Russian language.'

'Is this Baron a bit of a pedant?' asked Alexandra Pavlovna.

'Not at all, ma'am; Darya Mikhaylovna says that, on the contrary, he can be immediately recognized as a man of refinement. He spoke with such eloquence of Beethoven that even the old Prince became excited ... I confess I'd like to have heard him myself: that's in my line, after all. Permit me to offer you this beautiful wild flower.'

Alexandra Pavlovna took the flower and after a few steps dropped it. In a couple of hundred steps, no more, she would be home. The newly built and newly whitewashed house, with its wide bright windows, looked out welcomingly from the thick green foliage of ancient limes and maples.

'So how, ma'am, would you like me to inform Darya Mikhaylovna,' Pandalevsky began, slightly offended by the fate of the flower he had proffered, 'will you be coming to dinner? Her ladyship asks both you and your dear brother.'

'Yes, we'll come, without fail. How is Natasha?'

'Natalya Alexeyevna is very well, ma'am, thank God ... But we've already passed the turning to Darya Mikhaylovna's estate. Permit me now to take leave of you.'

Alexandra Pavlovna stopped.

'Surely you're coming to us, aren't you?' she inquired in an irresolute voice.

'I would heartily like to, ma'am, but I'm afraid of being late. Darya Mikhaylovna is pleased to hear a new *étude* by Thalberg,[3] so I must practise it and learn it. What is more, I must confess I doubt whether my conversation would give you any pleasure.'

'Oh, but ... why should you ...'

Pandalevsky sighed and expressively lowered his eyes.

'Good-bye, Alexandra Pavlovna!' he said after a moment's silence, bowed, and took a step backwards.

Alexandra Pavlovna turned about and went home.

Konstantin Diomidych also set off on his way. All the amiability instantly vanished from his face, to be replaced by a self-confident, almost austere expression. Even his walk changed; he no longer minced but took broader and heavier strides. He went a mile and a half breezily waving his cane, and suddenly the grin returned to his face: beside the track he saw a young, fairly pretty, peasant girl who was driving calves out of the oats. Konstantin Diomidych approached her as cautiously as a cat and started talking. At first she said nothing, crimsoned and giggled, then hid her mouth behind her sleeve, turned away and muttered:

'Go away, sir, do . . .'

Konstantin Diomidych shook his finger at her and ordered her to bring him some cornflowers.

'What d'you want flowers for, sir? Just to make a garland, is it?' the girl retorted. 'No, go away, sir, do . . .'

'Listen, my lovely little beauty . . .' Konstantin Diomidych was saying.

'Go away,' the girl interrupted him, 'the little masters are coming.'

Konstantin Diomidych glanced round. True enough, along the track came running Vanya and Petya, Darya Mikhaylovna's sons; behind them walked their teacher, Basistov, a young man of twenty-two who had only just completed his university course. Basistov was of robust build, with a simple face, a large nose, thick lips, and small porcine eyes, ugly and awkward, but kind-hearted, honest, and direct. He dressed casually and let his hair grow long not because he wanted to be in fashion but out of laziness; he was fond of eating and sleeping, but he also liked a good book and lively conversation, and he despised Pandalevsky from the depths of his heart.

Darya Mikhaylovna's children adored Basistov and were quite unafraid of him; he was on terms of intimacy with everyone else in the house, which did not entirely please the lady of the house no matter how much she went on about how prejudice did not exist for her.

'How do you do, my darling boys!' said Konstantin Diomidych. 'What an early walk you're having today! I,' he added, turning to Basistov, 'have been out some while; it's a passion of mine to enjoy the delights of nature.'

'We saw how you were enjoying the delights of nature,' Basistov muttered.

'You're a materialist: at once you're thinking God knows what. I know your s-sort.'

Whenever he spoke to Basistov or people like him, Pandalevsky became slightly irritated and tended to pronounce the letter *s* very clearly, even with a little hissing whistle.

'So I suppose you were just asking the girl the way, nothing else?' said Basistov, shifting his eyes right and left. He felt Pandalevsky looking him straight in the face and found this extremely unpleasant.

'I repeat: you're a materialist and nothing else. You deliberately want to see only the prosaic side of things . . .'

'Boys!' Basistov suddenly shouted, 'see that willow in the meadow, let's see who can run to it first . . . One! Two! Three!'

And the boys raced off to the willow. Basistov dashed after them.

'What a peasant!' thought Pandalevsky. 'He'll spoil those boys . . . A perfect peasant!'

And, with a self-satisfied glance at his own neat and elegant little figure, Konstantin Diomidych tapped the sleeve of his jacket a couple of times with outspread fingers, straightened his collar and went on his way. When he reached his room, he put on an ancient dressing-gown and seated himself at the piano with a preoccupied look.

II

THE house of Darya Mikhaylovna Lasunsky was regarded as being among the very finest in the whole of — province. Enormous, stone-built, constructed according to Rastrelli[1] drawings in the taste of the previous century, it rose majestically on the summit of a hill at whose foot flowed one of the chief rivers of central Russia. Darya Mikhaylovna herself was an aristocratic and wealthy lady, the widow of a privy councillor. Although Pandalevsky had been used to saying of her that she knew all Europe, and Europe, mind you, knew her as well! – still, Europe knew little of her and even in St Petersburg she played an unimportant role; but in Moscow everyone knew her and paid calls on her. She belonged to high society and had a reputation for being a slightly odd woman, not entirely nice but unusually clever. In her youth she had possessed very good looks. Poets had written her verses, young men had regularly fallen in love with her, important persons had courted her. But since that time some twenty-five or thirty years had passed and there remained not a trace of her former charms. 'Could it be,' someone seeing her for the first time would be bound to ask himself, 'could it be this thin, yellowish, sharp-nosed woman, still far from elderly, who was once such a beauty? Could it be she, this very woman, about whom the lyres were plucked? . . .' And he would inwardly wonder at the transitoriness of all earthly things. True, Pandalevsky found that Darya Mikhaylovna's magnificent eyes had retained their astonishing brilliance; but then it was Pandalevsky who maintained that all Europe knew her.

Each summer Darya Mikhaylovna used to travel to her country estate with her children (she had three of them: a daughter Natalya, seventeen, and two sons of ten and nine) and live openly – that is to say she would welcome men, particularly bachelors, as her guests; the ladies of the provinces she couldn't endure. And the things that used to be said about her by these ladies! According to them, Darya Mikhaylovna was both arrogant and immoral, and a frightful tyrant of a woman; but, worst of all, she allowed herself such liberties in her conversation that it was quite horrifying! As a matter of fact, Darya Mikhaylovna did not like confining herself in any way in the country, and in the unaffected freedom of her behaviour could be discerned a faint suggestion of the metropolitan lioness's disdain for the fairly uncultured and shallow beings who surrounded her ... She would also behave very freely, even sarcastically, towards her townee acquaintances, but there was no suggestion of disdain in her manner.

Has the reader not noticed, by the way, that a man who is unusually free and easy in the company of his inferiors is never free and easy with his superiors? Why should this be so? However, this kind of question gets one nowhere.

When Konstantin Diomidych Pandalevsky, having eventually learned the Thalberg *étude*, came down to the drawing-room from his own clean and cheerful room, he found the entire company of the house already assembled. The *salon* had already begun. On a broad couch, with her legs tucked under her and displaying in her hands a new French brochure, was the lady of the house; by the window sitting at their embroidery were, on the one hand, Darya Mikhaylovna's daughter and, on the other, Mlle Boncourt, her governess, an elderly and dry old thing of about sixty, with a black hairpiece under a colourful mob-cap, and cotton wool stuffed in her ears; in the corner, beside the door, was Basistov reading a newspaper, next to him Petya and Vanya were playing draughts, and leaning against the stove with his hands behind his back was a gentleman of medium height with dishevelled grey hair, a swarthy face, and active dark little eyes – a certain Afrikan Semyonych Pigasov.

An odd fellow was this Pigasov. Embittered against each

and everyone – particularly against women – he criticized from morn to night, sometimes very aptly, sometimes rather obtusely, but always with enjoyment. His irritability used to go to childish lengths; his laugh, the sound of his voice, his whole being seemed to be saturated in bile. Darya Mikhaylovna was always glad to receive Pigasov: he amused her with his witticisms. They were indeed on the amusing side. It was his passion to exaggerate everything. For example: no matter what misfortune was being discussed – they might be telling him that lightning had set fire to a village, that water had flooded into a mill, that a peasant had cut off his hand with his axe – he would ask each time with concentrated bitterness: 'And what is her name?' – that is, what's the woman called who caused the misfortune, because he was certain that a woman would be at the bottom of every misfortune if only one took the trouble to plumb the matter to its depths. He once flung himself on to his knees before a lady he scarcely knew, who was offering him something to eat, and began tearfully, but with rage written all over his face, to implore her to have mercy on him, that he had done her no wrong and would never impose himself on her again. Once a horse raced down a hill with one of Darya Mikhaylovna's laundry-maids, overturned her into a ditch, and almost killed her. From that moment Pigasov never called that horse anything but 'a nice, nice gee-gee' and found the hill and the ditch exceptionally picturesque spots. Pigasov had been unlucky in his life – and he consequently put on these outlandish airs. He came of poor parents. His father had held various small posts, was hardly literate and gave no thought to his son's education: he fed and clothed him – and that was all. His mother made much of him, but soon died. Pigasov set about educating himself, enrolled himself at the local school, then at the high school, taught himself languages, French, German, and even Latin, and, having left high school with excellent testimonials, set off for Dorpat,[2] where he had a continual struggle with poverty, but stayed the three-year course to the end. Pigasov's capabilities were not out of the ordinary; he distinguished himself by his patience and perseverance, but particularly marked in him was a feeling of ambition, a desire to find a place for himself in good society, not to fall behind, to spite fate. He had studied earnestly and entered the University of Dorpat driven on by ambition. Poverty angered him and cultivated in him keen powers of observation and cunning. He expressed himself very much in his own way; from his youth onwards he had evolved his own brand of bilious and irascible rhetoric. His ideas never rose above the commonplace; yet he talked in such a way that he could seem not only clever, but even a very clever man. Having obtained his candidate's degree,[3] Pigasov decided to devote himself to an academic life: he realized that in any other career he would have no chance of keeping up with his fellow students (he tried to choose them from among the well-to-do and knew how to pass as one of them, even flattered them, though he never ceased his criticism for a moment). But at this point, to put it simply, there just wasn't enough of the right material in him. Self-taught, but with no love of learning, at bottom Pigasov knew too little. He failed cruelly in his defence of his dissertation, while another student who shared the same room, at whom he was constantly laughing, an extremely limited man but one who had received a proper and solid education, was completely successful. This failure infuriated Pigasov: he threw all his books and notes in the fire and entered the civil service. At first, things went well enough: he made a splendid official, not very efficient, but extremely self-confident and lively: but he wanted to find a place for himself at once in the best society – got himself involved in a shady business, came a cropper, and was forced into retirement. For three years he sat at home in a little village he had luckily acquired and suddenly married a rich, half-educated girl from a merchant's family whom he had hooked with his familiar and sarcastic ways. But Pigasov's character had already become too irritable and embittered and he found family life oppressive . . . His wife, after living with him a few years, left secretly for Moscow and sold her estate to a clever speculator, just when Pigasov had finished building a mansion on it. Shaken to the roots of his being by this last blow, Pigasov embarked on litigation with his wife but gained nothing . . . He was now living out his life alone, travelling round to neighbours whom he abused up to their eyes and even to their faces and who always received him with a kind of forced half-laugh, although he never seriously frightened them – and he forgot all about books. He had about a hundred serfs; his peasants lived well enough.

'Ah! Constantin!' exclaimed Darya Mikhaylovna, as soon as Pandalevsky entered the drawing-room. 'Will Alexandrine be coming?'

'Alexandra Pavlovna ordered me to thank your ladyship and to say that she considers it a particular pleasure,' responded Konstantin Diomidych, bowing pleasantly on all sides and gently raising a plump, white little hand with pointed fingernails to hair that had been superbly groomed.

'And will Volyntsev also be coming?'

'Yes, your ladyship.'

'So Afrikan Semyonich,' Darya Mikhaylovna went on, turning to Pigasov, 'in your opinion, young ladies do not know how to behave naturally?'

Pigasov's lips twisted to one side and he gave a nervous jerk of his elbow.

'I say,' he began slowly (when assailed by a very strong attack of loathing he always spoke slowly and distinctly), 'I say that young ladies generally – naturally I am not speaking about present company . . .'

'But that doesn't stop you from thinking about them,' Darya Mikhaylovna interrupted.

'I am not talking about them,' Pigasov repeated. 'All young ladies generally behave unnaturally in the highest degree, especially in the expression of their feelings. A young lady, say, is frightened, or delighted by something, or saddened, and she will at once assume some kind of elegant twist in her whole body' (and Pigasov most ungracefully arched his back and spread out his arms) 'and only then will she cry: Ah! or laugh or cry. However, I did once succeed' (and here Pigasov gave a self-satisfied smile) 'in obtaining a true, unfeigned expression of feeling from one remarkably unnatural young lady!'

'In what way?'

Pigasov's eyes began to sparkle.

'I struck her on the behind with an aspen stick. As soon as she screeched I cried: "Bravo! Bravo! That was your true voice of nature, that was a natural cry of pain. That's how you should always behave in future."'

Everyone laughed.

'What nonsense you do talk, Afrikan Semyonych!' exclaimed Darya Mikhaylovna. 'I can hardly believe you'd poke a stick at a young girl!'

'Yes, indeed, a stick, a regular stave, like the kind they use to defend castles.'

'*Mais c'est une horreur ce que vous dites là, Monsieur,*' shrieked Mlle Boncourt, looking round threateningly at the children who were in fits of laughter.

'You mustn't believe him,' said Darya Mikhaylovna. 'Surely you know what he's like, don't you?'

But the vexed Frenchwoman took a long time to calm herself and went on muttering something under her breath.

'You may not believe me,' Pigasov went on cold-bloodedly, 'but I maintain I've told the absolute truth and nothing but the truth. Who should know if not I? After this you'll most probably not believe me that our neighbour Chepuzov, Yelena Antonovna, told me herself – herself, mind you – how she'd done in her own nephew.[4] You won't, will you?'

'It's just another of your stories!'

'So be it, so be it! Listen and then judge for yourselves. Mind you, I have no wish to slander her, I even like her, insofar as it's possible to like a woman, that is. She hasn't got a single book in her house, except the church calendar, and she can only read that out loud – the effort makes her break into a sweat and she complains that her eyes feel as though they're out on stalks ... In short, she's a good woman and her servants are well fed. Why should I tell tales about her?'

'Well, there you are!' remarked Darya Mikhaylovna. 'Afrikan Semyonych's on his hobby-horse again and he'll be there till nightfall.'

'My hobby-horse indeed ... Women have as many as three of them from which they never get down – unless they're asleep.'

'What are these three hobby-horses?'

'Their names are Needle, Nag, and Nark.'

'You know something, Afrikan Semyonych,' began Darya Mikhaylovna, 'there must be some reason why you're so embittered against women. One of them must have ...'

'Hurt my feelings, you want to say?' Pigasov interrupted her.

Darya Mikhaylovna was a little put out; she recalled Pigasov's unfortunate marriage and simply gave a nod of the head.

'One woman certainly did hurt my feelings,' said Pigasov, 'though she was a kind woman, very kind ...'

'Who was she?'

'My mother,' said Pigasov in a low voice.

'Your mother? How could she have hurt your feelings?'

'By giving birth to me ...'

Darya Mikhaylovna frowned.

'It seems to me,' she began, 'our conversation has taken an unhappy turn ... Constantin, play us the new Thalberg *étude*. Perhaps the sound of music will soften Afrikan Semyonych's feelings. Orpheus, after all, tamed wild beasts with his music.'

Konstantin Diomidych sat down at the piano and gave a

very satisfying rendering of the *étude*. At first Natalya Alexe-yevna listened with interest, but after a while she again took up her work.

'*Merci, c'est charmant,*' said Darya Mikhaylovna. 'I do like Thalberg. *Il est si distingué.* What's made you so thoughtful, Afrikan Semyonych?'

'I am thinking,' Pigasov began slowly, 'that there are three categories of egoist: egoists who live and let live; egoists who live and do not let live; and finally egoists who do not live and do not let others live ... Women for the most part be-long to the third category.'

'How charming that is! One thing only surprises me, Afrikan Semyonych – how self-confident you are in your judgements, as if you could never make a mistake!'

'Whoever said such a thing! I can also make a mistake, a man can make a mistake. But do you know what the differ-ence is between a mistake made by a man and one made by a woman? You don't? It's this: a man could, for instance, say that twice two is not four but five or three and a half, but a woman will say that twice two is – a stearin candle.'

'I think I've heard that one from you before ... Tell me, though, what connection has your idea about the three cate-gories of egoist with the music you've just heard?'

'None. I wasn't listening.'

'Well, my man, you are incorrigible, though it's no mat-ter,'[5] responded Darya Mikhaylovna, slightly misquoting a line from Griboyedov. 'What are you fond of if you don't like music? Literature perhaps?'

'I'm fond of literature but not present-day literature.'

'Why?'

'This is why. I was recently crossing the Oka on a ferry with some gent or other. The ferry reached a steep landing-stage: the carriages had to be manhandled onto land. This gent had an extremely heavy carriage. While the ferrymen hauled it up onto the bank, the gent, standing on the ferry, was grunting and groaning so much one even felt sorry for him ... Well, that, I thought, is a novel application of the system of division of labour! Present-day literature's just like that: others do the heavy work of heaving and shoving, while it does the grunting and groaning.'

Darya Mikhaylovna smiled.

'And it's called reproduction of contemporary reality,' the irrepressible Pigasov went on, 'profound feeling for social questions, and so on ... What a lot of high-sounding words!'

'At least women, whom you attack so much, don't use high-sounding words.'

Pigasov gave a shrug.

'They don't use them because they don't know how to.'

Darya Mikhaylovna crimsoned slightly.

'You're beginning to be insolent, Afrikan Semyonych!' she remarked with a forced smile.

Everything became quiet in the room.

'Where is Zolotonosha?' one of the boys asked Basistov.

'In the province of Poltava, dear boy,' Pigasov chimed in, 'in Double-Dutch Land, the Ukraine.' (He was delighted by the opportunity to change the subject.) 'We were just talking about literature,' he went on, 'and if I had any spare cash I'd immediately transform myself into a Ukrainian poet.'

'What are you talking about? A fine poet you'd make!' retorted Darya Mikhaylovna. 'Do you know any Ukrainian?'

'None at all, and it's really quite unnecessary.'

'How is it unnecessary?'

'It's unnecessary in this way. You only have to take a sheet of paper and write at the top: *Meditation*, and then begin: "With a hey and a ho, You're my fate, you're my woe!" or: "Cossack Nalivayko sat down on a tump!' followed by: "Down by the hill, down by the green, with a rumpty-tum-tum, rumpty-tum-tum, and a hey and a ho!' or something like that. And it's in the bag! Print it and publish it. Your

Ukrainian'll read it, rest his chin on his hand and burst into tears without fail – he's such a sensitive soul!'

'Do you mind!' exclaimed Basistov. 'What on earth are you saying? It's beyond all reason. I've lived in the Ukraine, I love the Ukraine and I know its language ... "Rumpty-tum-tum, rumpty-tum-tum" is complete nonsense.'

'That's as may be, but your Ukrainian'll still burst into tears. You mentioned the language ... Is there a Ukrainian language? I once asked a native of the region to translate the following sentence – it happened to be the first one that came to mind; Grammar is the art of reading and writing correctly. Do you know, this is how he translated it: Grammaire iz ye arte of readinge and writinge correctlie ... Do you call that a language? A language in its own right? Sooner than agree to that, I'd let my best friend be boiled in oil ...'

Basistov wanted to protest.

'Leave him alone,' said Darya Mikhaylovna. 'You must surely know that you'll hear nothing from him except paradoxes.'

Pigasov smiled caustically. A footman entered and announced the arrival of Alexandra Pavlovna and her brother.

Darya Mikhaylovna rose to meet her guests.

'How do you do, Alexandrine!' she began, going up to her. 'How thoughtful of you to come ... How do you do, Sergey Pavlych!'

Volyntsev pressed Darya Mikhaylovna's hand and went over to Natalya Alexeyevna.

'And is the new acquaintance of yours, this Baron, likely to be coming today?' asked Pigasov.

'Yes, he'll be coming.'

'He's reputed to be a great philosophe, literally fizzing with Hegel.'

Darya Mikhaylovna did not respond but seated Alexandra Pavlovna on the couch and settled herself beside her.

'Philosophy,' Pigasov continued, 'is the highest point of

47

view! These high points of view will be the death of me. And what on earth can one see from a high point? Suppose you wanted to buy a horse, you wouldn't start looking at it from up a watch tower!'

'Did this Baron want to bring you an essay of his?' asked Alexandra Pavlovna.

'Yes, an article,' answered Darya Mikhaylovna with exaggerated nonchalance, 'about the relations between trade and industry in Russia . . . But don't be scared: we won't read it here . . . I didn't ask you to come for that. *Le baron est aussi aimable que savant.* And he speaks Russian so well! *C'est un vrai torrent . . . il vous entraîne.'*

'He speaks Russian so well,' grumbled Pigasov, 'that he merits praise in French.'

'You may grumble, Afrikan Semyonych, you may grumble . . . it goes very well with your dishevelled hair-style . . . Still, does it matter if he isn't coming? You know what, *messieurs et mesdames,*' added Darya Mikhaylovna, glancing round her, 'let's go into the garden . . . There's an hour or so until dinner and the weather's perfect . . .'

The entire company rose and went into the garden.

Darya Mikhaylovna's garden extended right down to the river. It had many paths lined with old limetrees, dark as old gold and full of fragrance, with emerald gleams of light at the end of them, and many arbours of acacia and lilac.

Volyntsev, in the company of Natalya and Mlle Boncourt, made his way into the very depths of the garden. Volyntsev walked beside Natalya and said nothing. Mlle Boncourt followed a little way behind.

'What have you been doing today?' Volyntsev asked eventually, pulling at the ends of his fine dark-brown moustache. In the features of his face he closely resembled his sister; but there was less playfulness and vivacity in them and his eyes, handsome and tender though they were, somehow looked sad.

48

'Nothing really,' Natalya answered. 'I've listened to Pigasov's invective, done some embroidery, and read.'

'What've you been reading?'

'I've been reading . . . a history of the crusades,' said Natalya with a slight hesitation in her speech.

Volyntsev looked towards her.

'Ah!' he exclaimed after a pause. 'That must have been interesting.'

He broke off a small branch and began twisting it about in the air. They walked about another twenty steps.

'What sort of a person is this Baron whom your mother's got to know?' Once again Volyntsev opened the conversation with a question.

'A Kammerjunker, on a visit; *maman* speaks very highly of him.'

'Your dear mother can be easily carried away.'

'That shows she is still young in heart,' Natalya remarked.

'Yes, of course. I'll soon be sending you your horse. It is almost completely broken in. I want it to start at a gallop and I'll get it to do that.'

'*Merci* . . . But I have a bad conscience about it. You're breaking it in yourself . . . they say that's very difficult . . .'

'In order to give you the slightest pleasure, you know, Natalya Alexeyevna, I'm prepared . . . I'm . . . and not just small matters like this . . .'

Volyntsev lost his way.

Natalya glanced at him sympathetically and once again said: '*Merci.*'

'You know,' Sergey Pavlych continued after a long silence, 'that there's not a single thing . . . But what am I saying this for! You already know it all.'

At that moment a bell sounded in the house.

'*Ah! la cloche du dîner!*' cried Mlle Boncourt. '*Rentrons.*'

'*Quel dommage,*' reflected the aged Frenchwoman as she made her way up the balcony steps in the wake of Volyntsev and Natalya, *'quel dommage que ce charmant garçon ait si peu de ressources dans la conversation . . .'* which could be translated as: 'You're a nice fellow, but a bit slow.'

The Baron did not arrive for dinner. They waited about half an hour.

At table the conversation was sticky. Sergey Pavlych simply kept on giving Natalya looks as he sat next to her and kept on attentively replenishing her glass of water. Pandalevsky carefully strove to charm his neighbour, Alexandra Pavlovna: he bubbled over with sweet words while she could scarcely keep from yawning.

Basistov rolled little pellets of bread and thought about nothing; even Pigasov was silent and, when Darya Mikhaylovna remarked to him that he was very grumpy today, he answered sombrely: 'When am I not grumpy? It's my business to be grumpy . . .' and, with a bitter grin, added: 'You won't have to wait long. I'm just your honest home-made brew, your simple Russian kvass, whereas your Kammerjunker's . . .'

'Bravo!' cried Darya Mikhaylovna, 'Pigasov's jealous, jealous beforehand!'

But Pigasov made no response to her and simply looked morose.

It struck seven and the entire company again assembled in the drawing-room.

'Obviously he's not coming,' said Darya Mikhaylovna.

At which moment the noise of a carriage was heard and a small tarantass drove into the courtyard, and after a few moments a footman entered the drawing-room and handed Darya Mikhaylovna a letter on a small silver tray. She ran her eyes over it and, turning to the footman, asked:

'Where is the gentleman who brought this letter?'

'Sitting in the carriage, your ladyship. Do you wish him to come in?'

'Ask him to come in.'

The footman went out.

'Imagine, how annoying,' Darya Mikhaylovna continued, 'the Baron has just received an order to return at once to St Petersburg. He has sent me his article with a certain Mr Rudin, his friend. The Baron wanted to introduce him to me – he has a very high opinion of him. But how annoying this is! I'd hoped the Baron would spend a few days here . . .'

'Dmitry Nikolayevich Rudin,' the footman announced.

III

THERE entered a man of about thirty-five, tall, slightly round-shouldered, curly-haired, swarthy, with irregular, but expressive and intelligent features and a liquid brilliance in his lively dark-blue eyes, with a straight broad nose and finely chiselled lips. What he wore was not new and looked tight, just as if he had grown out of it.

He walked gingerly up to Darya Mikhaylovna and, giving a slight bow, told her that he had long wished to have the honour of being introduced to her and that his friend, the Baron, greatly regretted that he was unable to say good-bye in person.

The high-pitched sound of Rudin's voice was out of keeping with his stature and broad chest.

'Do sit down . . . I'm very glad,' said Darya Mikhaylovna and, having made the introductions, asked him if he lived in the region or was visiting.

'My estate is in T— province,' answered Rudin, holding his hat on his knees, 'and I've only come here recently. I came on business and for the time being I'm staying in your local town.'

'With whom?'

'With the doctor. He's an old university friend.'

'Ah, at the doctor's! . . . People speak highly of him. They say he knows his job. Have you known the Baron for long?'

'I met him last winter in Moscow and I've just spent a week or so with him.'

'He's a very clever person – the Baron.'

'Yes, ma'am.'

Darya Mikhaylovna sniffed the corner of a handkerchief that had been dipped in eau de cologne.

'Are you in government service?' she asked.

'Who? I, ma'am?'

'Yes.'

'No ... I'm retired.'

A short silence ensued. The general conversation was again revived.

'Permit me to inquire,' began Pigasov, turning to Rudin, 'are you familiar with the content of the article which the Herr Baron has sent?'

'It is known to me.'

'The article is about the relationship of trade ... or, no, forgive me, of industry to trade in our fatherland ... I believe that's how you expressed it, Darya Mikhaylovna?'

'Yes, it is about that,' said Darya Mikhaylovna and pressed a hand to her brow.

'I am, of course, a poor judge in these matters,' went on Pigasov, 'but I must confess that to me the very title of the article seems extraordinarily ... how can I put it delicately? ... extraordinarily obscure and confused.'

'Why does it seem to you like that?'

Pigasov grinned and directed a glance at Darya Mikhaylovna.

'It's quite clear to you, then?' he said, again turning his foxy little face towards Rudin.

'To me? Yes.'

'Hmm ... Of course, you're in a better position to know.'

'Have you a headache?' Alexandra Pavlovna asked Darya Mikhaylovna.

'No. It's just that I have ... *C'est nerveux*.'

'Permit me to inquire,' Pigasov began again in his little nasal voice, 'your acquaintance, Herr Baron Mueffel ... that's his name, I believe?'

'Precisely so.'

'Herr Baron Mueffel is specially concerned with political economy or is it simply that he devotes to this interesting science only the hours of leisure remaining from time spent in social pleasures and in the office?'

Rudin looked intently at Pigasov.

'The Baron is a dilettante in the matter,' he answered, slightly colouring, 'but his article has much that is just and interesting in it.'

'I can't argue with you, not knowing the article ... But, dare I ask, does the work by your friend, Baron Mueffel, take more account, perhaps, of generalizations than of facts?'

'It contains both facts and generalizations based on facts.'

'I see, I see. I must make it known to you that in my opinion ... and I can, I think, in the circumstances, have my say, after having been for three years at Dorpat ... all these so-called generalizations, all your hypotheses and systems ... forgive me, I'm a provincial, I call a spade a spade ... are of no use whatever. It's all just so much intellectualizing – just a way of pulling wool over people's eyes. Give us facts, gentlemen, that's all we want from you.'

'Well I never!' protested Rudin. 'And is there no need to give the sense of the facts?'

'Generalizations!' Pigasov went on. 'These generalizations, overall views, conclusions will be the death of me! They're all based on so-called convictions; everyone talks about his convictions, and he goes around with them expecting them to be respected, what is more ... Bah!'

And Pigasov shook his fist in the air. Pandalevsky burst out laughing.

'Excellent,' said Rudin. 'Then according to you there are no convictions?'

'No, they don't exist.'

'That's your conviction?'

'Yes.'

'Then how can you say they don't exist? There's one for you to start with.'

Everyone in the room smiled and exchanged glances.

'Allow me, allow me, however . . .' Pigasov was beginning. But Darya Mikhaylovna clapped her hands, exclaimed: 'Bravo, bravo, Pigasov's been beaten!' – and ever so gently took Rudin's hat from his hands.

'Wait a moment before rejoicing, your ladyship: you won't have to wait long!' said Pigasov with vexation. 'It's not sufficient to make a witty remark with a look of superiority: you have to demonstrate, to disprove . . . We've lost sight of the point of our discussion.'

'Allow me to say,' remarked Rudin coldly, 'that the whole thing is very simple. You don't believe in the value of generalizations, you don't believe in convictions . . .'

'I do not believe, I do not believe, I don't believe in a thing!'

'Very good. You're a sceptic.'

'I don't see the need to use such a learned term. Besides . . .'

'Please don't interrupt so!' interposed Darya Mikhaylovna.

'Bite him, go on, bite him!' Pandalevsky said to himself at that instant and grinned all over his face.

'The term expresses what I meant,' Rudin continued. 'You know what it means, so why not use it? You don't believe in a thing . . . then why do you believe in facts?'

'Why? That's marvellous! Facts are a known quantity, everyone knows what facts are . . . I can tell what they are from experience, from my own feelings.'

'As if your feelings can never deceive you! Your feeling tells you that the sun goes round the earth – or perhaps you don't agree with Copernicus? Perhaps you don't believe even in him?'

A fleeting smile again appeared on everyone's face and all eyes were directed at Rudin. 'This man is not stupid,' was everyone's thought.

'You will go on joking,' said Pigasov. 'Of course, this is very original, but it is beside the point.'

'In everything that I have so far said,' Rudin protested,

'there is unfortunately far too little originality. It is all very old stuff and has been said a thousand times already. The point is . . .'

'Exactly what is it?' asked Pigasov not without a certain insolence. In an argument he always began by making fun of his opponent, then became rude and ended up by sulking and falling silent.

'The point is,' Rudin went on, 'I have to admit I cannot but feel sincere regret when I find intelligent people attacking . . .'

'Systems?' interrupted Pigasov.

'Yes, if you wish – attacking systems. What frightens you so much about that word? Every system is based on a knowledge of the fundamental laws, the essential laws of life . . .'

'But you can never know what they are, you can never discover them, for pity's sake!'

'I dare say. Of course, not everyone can know them and to err is human. But you will no doubt agree with me that Newton, for instance, has discovered at least some of the fundamental laws. Granted that he was a genius; but the discoveries of geniuses are great precisely because they become accessible to all. The striving to seek out the common element in particular phenomena is one of the basic attributes of the human mind, and the essence of our entire civilization.'

'Now look where you're off to!' broke in Pigasov in a blasé voice. 'I'm a practical chap and I don't go in for all these metaphysical refinements and I don't want to.'

'Excellent! That's for you to decide. But you should note that your very desire to be exclusively a practical chap is its own form of system or theory . . .'

'Our entire civilization! you say,' Pigasov chimed in, 'another thing you've tried to startle us with! A lot of good it is, this much-vaunted civilization! I wouldn't give you a brass farthing for your civilization!'

'But how badly you argue, Afrikan Semyonych!' remarked Darya Mikhaylovna, inwardly extremely pleased by the composure and elegant good manners of her new acquaintance. '*C'est un homme comme il faut*,' she thought, glancing with warm attentiveness into Rudin's face. 'He must be cultivated.' These last words she mentally uttered to herself in Russian.

'I don't intend to defend civilization,' Rudin continued after a short pause. 'It doesn't need me to defend it. You don't like it . . . every man to his own tastes. Besides, it would take us too far from the point. Allow me just to remind you of the ancient saying: "You are angry, O Jupiter, then you must be in the wrong." I wanted to say that all these attacks on systems, on generalizations and so on are particularly distressing because, together with systems, people are denying knowledge in general, science, and faith in science – and, at the same time, faith in themselves and their own powers. But people need this faith: they cannot live on impressions alone, and it is wrong for them to fear ideas and not trust them. Scepticism has always distinguished itself by barrenness and impotence . . .'

'It's all so many words!' muttered Pigasov.

'Perhaps. But let me point out to you that in saying: "It's all so many words!" we are frequently ourselves wishing to avoid the necessity of saying something more to the point.'

'Such as?' asked Pigasov and screwed up his eyes.

'You've understood my meaning,' Rudin retorted with an involuntary but immediately restrained impatience. 'I repeat, if a man has no firm principle in which he believes, if he has no ground on which he stands firmly, how can he assess the needs, the significance, and the future of his people? How can he know what he must do, if . . .?'

'Have a seat!' Pigasov declared abruptly, bowed and retreated, not looking at anyone.

Rudin gave him a look, smiled slightly, and fell silent.

'Aha! He's run away!' said Darya Mikhaylovna. 'Don't worry, Dmitry . . . Forgive me,' she added with a welcoming smile, 'your patronymic?'

'Nikolaich.'

'Don't worry, dear Dmitry Nikolaich! He hasn't deceived any of us. He wants to give the impression that he doesn't *want* to continue the argument but he knows in his heart he *can't*. Do come a little closer and we can have a chat.'

Rudin drew his chair forward.

'How is it that we haven't met before?' Darya Mikhaylovna went on. 'I'm very surprised ... Have you read this book? *C'est de Tocqueville, vous savez?*'

And Darya Mikhaylovna handed Rudin the French brochure.

Rudin took the little book, flipped through several pages and, replacing it on the table, answered that he had not read this particular work by de Tocqueville but had often considered the same question. A conversation was struck up. At first Rudin seemed to hesitate, was undecided about expressing himself, could not find the right words, but finally he caught alight and began speaking eloquently. Within a quarter of an hour his voice alone filled the room. The assembled company gathered round him in a circle.

Pigasov alone remained at a distance, in a corner beside the fireplace. Rudin spoke intelligently, passionately, and effectively; he exhibited much knowledge, a great deal of reading. No one had expected to find him a remarkable man ... He was so indifferently dressed, so little had been heard of him. To all of them it seemed incomprehensible and strange how someone so intelligent could pop up suddenly in the provinces. For this reason he came as that much more of a surprise to everyone and, if one may say so, more of a charmer, primarily to Darya Mikhaylovna ... She was proud of her new find and had already begun to think about how she might launch Rudin in high society. In her first impression there was much that was childish, notwithstanding her years. Alexandra Pavlovna, if the truth be told, understood little of what Rudin was saying, but she was astonished and delighted;

her brother was also amazed; Pandalevsky observed Darya Mikhaylovna's attitude and was envious; Pigasov thought: 'For 500 roubles I'd get you a better singing bird!' ... But most astounded of all were Basistov and Natalya. Basistov could scarcely draw breath; he sat all the while open-mouthed and pop-eyed – and listened, listened, as he had never listened to anyone in his whole life, and Natalya's face was covered in a crimson flush and her gaze, directed fixedly at Rudin, both darkened and glittered in turn ...

'What splendid eyes he has!' Volyntsev whispered to her.

'Yes.'

'It's such a pity his hands are large and red.'

Natalya made no response.

Tea was served. The conversation became more general, but if only through the very immediacy with which all grew quiet as soon as Rudin opened his mouth was it possible to judge the force of the impression which he made. Darya Mikhaylovna suddenly took it into her head to tease Pigasov. She went up to him and said in a low voice: 'Why are you saying nothing and merely smiling caustically? Come on, have another go at him' – and, without awaiting his reply, summoned Rudin with a wave of the hand.

'There's something else you don't know about him,' she said, pointing at Pigasov. 'He's a frightful women-hater, always attacking them; please direct him into the way of truth.'

Rudin looked at Pigasov – necessarily looked down at him because he was a couple of heads taller. Pigasov almost writhed with loathing and his bilious face turned white.

'Darya Mikhaylovna is mistaken,' he said unsteadily. 'It's not just women I attack: I have no great fondness for the whole human race.'

'What could have given you such a poor opinion of it?' asked Rudin.

Pigasov looked him straight in the eyes.

'Probably a study of my own heart in which I daily find more and more trash. I judge others by myself. Perhaps that is unjust, and I am genuinely much worse than others; but what do you suggest I do about it? It's a habit!'

'I understand you and sympathize with you,' responded Rudin. 'Is there a noble soul that hasn't experienced a thirst for self-humiliation? But one shouldn't remain in this parlous state.'

'I humbly thank you for awarding my soul a certificate of nobility,' retorted Pigasov, 'but my state is, well, not so bad, so that even if there were a way out of it, God be praised! I wouldn't start looking for it.'

'But that means, if you'll pardon the expression, a preference for satisfying your own egoism rather than a desire to be and to live in the truth . . .'

'Really!' exclaimed Pigasov. 'Egoism – that I can understand, and you, I hope, can understand, and everyone can understand; but truth – what is truth? Where is it, this truth?'

'I warn you that you're repeating yourself,' remarked Darya Mikhaylovna.

Pigasov gave a shrug of the shoulders.

'What's wrong with that? I am asking: where is the truth? Even philosophers don't know what it is. Kant says it's one thing; while Hegel says no, that's nonsense, it's another.'

'And do you know what it is Hegel says about it?' asked Rudin without raising his voice.

'I repeat,' went on a heated Pigasov, 'that I can't understand what truth is. In my view it doesn't exist at all on earth – that's to say, the word itself exists, but not the thing itself.'

'Fie, fie!' cried Darya Mikhaylovna. 'You ought to be ashamed to say that, you old sinner, you! No such thing as truth? After that what's the point in going on living?'

'I most certainly think, Darya Mikhaylovna,' replied Pigasov with annoyance, 'that it would be in any case a great deal easier for you to live without truth than without your cook Stepan, who is such a master at making Scotch broth! And what's the point of truth to you, kindly tell me? You can hardly make a mob-cap out of it!'

'A joke is no answer,' remarked Darya Mikhaylovna, 'especially when it borders on slander . . .'

'I don't know about the truth, but a true word evidently is not to your taste,' muttered Pigasov and retreated testily to his former place.

Rudin began speaking about egoistical ambition, and he began speaking very effectively. He argued that a man without ambition is a nonentity, that ambition was the lever of Archimedes with which the earth could be moved, but at the same time the only person who deserves the name of man is he who knows how to control his egoistical ambition, as a rider controls a horse, who can sacrifice self-interest to the general good . . .

'Egoism,' he concluded, 'is suicide. The egocentric man dries up like a solitary, barren tree; but egoism as an active aspiration to perfection is the source of all that is great . . . Yes! A man must destroy the stubborn egoism in his own personality, in order to give it the right to express itself!'

'Would you be good enough to lend me a pencil?' Pigasov addressed Basistov.

Basistov did not understand at once what Pigasov was asking him.

'What do you want a pencil for?' he eventually asked.

'I would like to note down Mr Rudin's last remark. If I don't, I'll most likely forget it – too bad! You will surely agree that such a remark is as good as a grand slam at cards.'

'There are certain things which it's wrong to laugh at and make fun of, Afrikan Semyonych!' said Basistov passionately and turned away from Pigasov.

Meanwhile Rudin went up to Natalya. She rose: her face expressed confusion.

Volyntsev, sitting next to her, also rose.

'I see there is a piano,' Rudin began softly and soothingly, like a prince on his travels. 'Is it you who play on it?'

'Yes, I do play,' said Natalya, 'but not very well. Konstantin Diomidych here plays much better than me.'

Pandalevsky thrust his face forward and bared his teeth in a grin.

'There's no need to say that, Natalya Alexeyevna: you do not play less well than me.'

'Do you know Schubert's *Erlkönig*?' asked Rudin.

'He knows it, he knows it!' chimed in Darya Mikhaylovna. 'Sit down, Constantin ... Are you fond of music, Dmitry Nikolaich?'

Rudin did no more than slightly incline his head and pass his hand over his hair as if preparing to listen. Pandalevsky began playing.

Natalya stood beside the piano, directly opposite Rudin. With the first chord his face took on a look of beauty. His dark-blue eyes wandered slowly, occasionally fixing on Natalya. Pandalevsky finished.

Rudin said nothing and went to the open window. A fragrant misty twilight lay like a soft shroud over the garden; the nearby trees breathed a dreamy freshness. Stars gleamed calmly. The summer night both basked and soothed. Rudin looked into the darkened garden – and turned round.

'The music and the night,' he said, 'reminded me of my time as a student in Germany, of our gatherings, our serenades ...'

'You were in Germany, then?' asked Darya Mikhaylovna.

'I spent a year in Heidelberg and about a year in Berlin.'

'Did you wear student dress? People say students dress there in a special way.'

'In Heidelberg I wore large boots with spurs and a short jacket with laces in place of buttons and grew my hair down to my shoulders ... In Berlin students dress like everyone else.'

'Tell us something about your student life,' said Alexandra Pavlovna softly.

Rudin began an anecdote. He was not entirely successful as a storyteller. His descriptions lacked colour. He did not know how to be humorous. However, Rudin soon moved from anecdotes about his foreign travels to statements about the significance of education and science, about universities and university life in general. With bold and sweeping flourishes he painted a panoramic picture. Everyone listened to him with profound attention. He spoke masterfully, and entertainingly, but not entirely lucidly . . . yet this very vagueness lent particular charm to his speech.

A profusion of ideas prevented Rudin from expressing himself cogently and precisely. Image after image poured out; analogies, now unexpectedly bold, now devastatingly apt, rose one after another. It was not with the complacent expertise of an experienced chatterbox, but with inspiration that his rushing impromptu speech was filled. He did not seek after words: they came obediently and freely to his lips and each word, it seemed, literally flowed straight from his soul and burned with all the heat of conviction. Rudin possessed what is almost the highest secret – the music of eloquence. By striking certain heart strings he could set all the others obscurely quivering and ringing. A listener might not understand precisely what was being talked about; but he would catch his breath, curtains would open wide before his eyes, something resplendent would burn dazzlingly ahead of him.

All Rudin's thoughts seemed to be directed towards the future; this lent them an air of impetuosity and youthfulness . . . Standing by the window, looking at no one in particular, he spoke, and, inspired by the general sympathy and attention, by the proximity of the young women, and the beauty of the night, carried away in the flow of his own feelings, he reached heights of eloquence and poetry . . . The very sound of his voice, quiet and intense, heightened the enchantment;

it seemed that some higher being spoke through his lips, to his own surprise ... Rudin spoke of what lends eternal significance to man's temporal existence.

'I remember a Scandinavian legend,'[1] he said in conclusion. 'A king is sitting with his warriors in a long, dark hall, around a fire. It takes place at night, in winter. Suddenly a small bird flies in through one open door and out at another. The king remarks that the little bird is like a man in this world: it flew out of the darkness and back into the darkness again, and did not stay long in the warmth and light ... "Oh, king," the eldest warrior objects, "the little bird will not lose itself in the dark but will find its nest." It is just like our life on earth that is so fleeting and insignificant; but everything great on earth is accomplished only by men. For man the awareness of being the instrument of these higher powers must take the place of all other joys: in death itself man will find his life, his nest ...'

Rudin stopped and lowered his eyes with an involuntary smile of embarrassment.

'*Vous êtes un poète,*' said Darya Mikhaylovna in a whisper.

And all inwardly agreed with her – all except Pigasov. Without awaiting the end of Rudin's long speech he very quietly took his hat and went out, having whispered maliciously to Pandalevsky who was standing by the door:

'No, it's not for me! I'm off to join the dunces!'

But no one stopped him going or noticed his absence.

The servants brought in supper and, half an hour later, all the guests had left on foot or in their carriages. Darya Mikhaylovna had persuaded Rudin to stay the night. Alexandra Pavlovna, returning home by carriage with her brother, several times started exclaiming with surprise at Rudin's unusual mind. Volyntsev usually agreed with her, yet he remarked that Rudin sometimes expressed himself a little obscurely ... that is, not entirely intelligibly, he added, wishing no doubt to clarify his thought; but his face darkened with a frown and his gaze, directed into a corner of the carriage, became even sadder.

Pandalevsky, going to bed and taking off his silk-embroidered braces, said aloud: 'A very skilful fellow!' – and suddenly, glaring at his servant-boy, ordered him out of the room. Basistov spent the whole night awake and dressed, writing a letter to a Moscow friend until dawn; while Natalya, although she both undressed and went to bed, also had no sleep and did not even close her eyes. Leaning her head on her hand, she looked intently into the darkness; the blood beat feverishly in her veins, and her bosom heaved frequently with a heavy sigh.

IV

THE next morning Rudin had only just got dressed when a
servant came from Darya Mikhaylovna with an invitation to
come to her study and have a cup of tea. Rudin found her
alone. She greeted him most warmly, inquired how he had
spent the night, herself poured him a cup of tea, even asking
whether she had given him enough sugar, offered him a cigarette and repeated at least a couple of times how surprised she
was that they had not met before. Rudin was on the point of
taking a seat a suitable distance from her, but Darya Mikhaylovna indicated a soft stool standing beside her armchair and,
slightly leaning towards him, began to question him about his
family, his intentions, and his plans. Darya Mikhaylovna
spoke nonchalantly and listened distractedly; but Rudin
understood only too well that she was flirting with him, even
flattering him. She would hardly otherwise have arranged
this morning rendezvous or have dressed so simply but ele-
gantly à la madame Récamier![1] No matter, Darya Mikhaylovna
soon stopped questioning him: she began telling him about
herself, about her own youth and the people she had known.
Rudin listened to her loquacity with interest, although –
strange to relate! – no matter who Darya Mikhaylovna talked
about she always remained in the foreground, she alone, and
the person in question always slipped into the background and
vanished. For his part, Rudin learned in detail what Darya
Mikhaylovna had said to such-and-such a high-ranking official
or what influence she had had on such-and-such an important
poet. Judging from Darya Mikhaylovna's stories one would
have thought that all the remarkable men of the last quarter
of a century had dreamed of nothing else except how to get
to know her or earn her esteem. She spoke of them quite
simply, without undue enthusiasm or praise, as intimates of

66

hers, calling some of them eccentrics. She spoke of them and, like a sumptuous setting for a precious stone, their names formed a glittering border for the chief name, that of Darya Mikhaylovna ...

Meantime Rudin listened, smoked, and was silent, save that occasionally he inserted some brief remarks into the garrulous lady's talk. He knew how to talk and was fond of talking; he had no aptitude for carrying on a conversation, but he knew how to listen. Anyone, whom he had not terrified out of his wits to start with, would trustingly become expansive in his presence, so keenly and encouragingly did he follow the thread of someone else's words. There was much warm-heartedness in him – that particular warmheartedness with which people are filled who are accustomed to feeling them-selves superior to others. In arguments he rarely allowed his opponent the chance to speak and would smother him beneath his rushing and impassioned dialectic.

Darya Mikhaylovna expressed herself in Russian. She prided herself on her knowledge of Russian, although gallic-isms and French words popped up in her speech frequently enough. She intentionally used simple folksy sayings, but not always successfully. Rudin's ear was not offended by the strange variety of speech forms on Darya Mikhaylovna's lips, and in any event he scarcely had an ear for such things.

Darya Mikhaylovna finally grew tired and, leaning back against her head-cushion in her armchair, directed her eyes at Rudin and fell silent.

'I now understand,' Rudin began slowly, 'I understand why you come each summer to the country. You need this rest: the peace of the countryside after life in the city refreshes and strengthens you. I'm sure you must have profound feeling for the beauties of nature.'

Darya Mikhaylovna looked askance at Rudin.

'Nature ... yes ... yes, of course ... I'm frightfully fond of it. But you know, Dmitry Nikolaich, even in the country you can't get by without people. And there's almost no one here. Pigasov's the most intelligent person here.'

'Yesterday's angry old man?' asked Rudin.

'Yes, him. Even he's all right for the country, though a bit of a laugh sometimes.'

'He is no fool,' responded Rudin, 'but he's on the wrong track. I don't know whether you'll agree with me, Darya Mikhaylovna, but there's nothing much to be gained from negation, from complete and universal negation. Criticize everything and you can easily pass for intelligent: that's a well-known trick. Well-disposed people are at once ready to conclude that you are above what you criticize. And this is often not so. In the first place, you can find a blemish in everything, and in the second place, even if you're talking sense, it's all the worse for you because your mind, directed only towards criticism, grows impoverished and dries up. In satisfying your egoism, you are depriving yourself of the real pleasures of perception; life, the essence of life, slips away from your petty and bilious observation and you end by barking loudly and making people laugh. To censure and criticize is a right to be enjoyed only by the man who genuinely loves.'

'*Voilà M. Pigassoff enterré,*' said Darya Mikhaylovna. 'What a master you are at defining people! Pigasov, however, would probably not understand you at all. And if he loves anything it's only himself.'

'And he criticizes himself in order to have the right to criticize others,' Rudin added.

Darya Mikhaylovna laughed.

'A case of the pot . . . how does the saying go? . . . a case of the kettle calling the pot black. By the way, what do you think of the Baron?'

'Of the Baron? He's a good chap with a kind heart and he knows a thing or two . . . but he lacks character. And all his life he'll remain part scholar, part man-of-the-world, a dilet-

68

tante in fact or, without mincing words – a nothing. It's a great pity!'

'I am of the same opinion,' responded Darya Mikhaylovna. 'I've read his article . . . *Entre nous . . . cela a assez peu de fond.*'

'Who else do you have here?' asked Rudin after a short silence.

Darya Mikhaylovna knocked the ash off her cigarette with her little finger.

'Almost no one. There is Alexandra Pavlovna Lipin whom you saw yesterday: she is very charming, but that's all. Her brother is also an excellent fellow, *un parfait honnête homme.* Prince Garin you know. That's all. There are one or two neighbours but they're of no importance. Either they give themselves all kinds of airs and graces and become frightfully pretentious, or they shy away from all company, or they simply know no bounds at all. I do not receive ladies, you know. There is another neighbour, reputed to be a very well-educated man, even a scholar, but an awful eccentric living in his own ivory tower. Alexandrine knows him and is not in-different to him, it seems . . . You should cultivate her, Dmitry Nikolaich. She's a charming person – she just needs a little cultivation, no more than that!'

'She is very likeable,' Rudin remarked.

'A perfect child, Dmitry Nikolaich, a real child. She was married, *mais c'est tout comme.* If I were a man I would only fall in love with women like that.'

'Is that really so?'

'Certainly. Such women are at least fresh, and you can't make a pretence of being fresh.'

'And of everything else you can?' asked Rudin and burst out laughing, which happened very rarely with him. When he laughed his face acquired an odd, almost elderly look, his eyes became puckered, his nose wrinkled.

'And who is this eccentric, as you call him, to whom Mrs Lipin is not indifferent?' he asked.

'A certain Mikhaylo Mikhaylych Lezhnev, a local landowner.'

Rudin was astounded and raised his head.

'Mikhaylo Mikhaylych Lezhnev,' he asked, 'is a neighbour of yours?'

'Yes. Do you know him?'

Rudin did not answer at once.

'I used to know him ... a long time ago. Surely, isn't he a rich man?' he added, picking at the fringe of his armchair.

'Yes, he's rich, although he dresses most frightfully and travels about everywhere in a racing droshky like any bailiff. I wanted to lure him over here: he's said to be clever. He and I have some business to discuss ... No doubt you know I manage my estate personally.'

Rudin nodded.

'Yes, I do so myself,' Darya Mikhaylovna went on. 'I am introducing no foreign nonsense, I am keeping to our own Russian way of doing things and, you see, things are not going badly,' she added, making a circling motion with her hand.

'I have always been convinced,' Rudin remarked politely, 'of the extreme injustice of those people who deny women any practical sense.'

Darya Mikhaylovna smiled pleasantly.

'You're very well disposed,' she said, 'but what on earth was it I wanted to say? What were we talking about? Oh, yes, about Lezhnev. I have some business about boundaries to discuss with him. I've invited him several times, and I'm even waiting for him today; but he doesn't come, God only knows why ... such an eccentric chap!'

The curtain before the door quietly parted and a butler entered, a tall, balding man with grey hair in a black frock-coat, white necktie, and white waistcoat.

'What do you want?' asked Darya Mikhaylovna and, turning slightly towards Rudin, said in a low voice: '*N'est-ce pas, comme il ressemble à Canning?*'[2]

'Mikhaylo Mikhaylych Lezhnev has arrived,' the butler announced. 'Do you wish to receive him?'

'Ah, my God!' exclaimed Darya Mikhaylovna. 'Talk of the devil! Ask him to come in!'

The butler went out.

'Such an eccentric chap, he's finally come, and just at the wrong time: he's interrupted our conversation.'

Rudin rose but Darya Mikhaylovna stopped him.

'Where are you off to? We can talk with you here. And I'd like you to define him as you did Pigasov. When you speak, *vous gravez comme avec un burin*. Do stay.'

Rudin was on the point of saying something, but thought a moment and stayed.

Mikhaylo Mikhaylych, who is already familiar to the reader, entered the study. He wore the same grey topcoat and in his sunburned hands he held the same old cap. He bowed calmly towards Darya Mikhaylovna and went up to the tea table.

'At last you've come to see us, Monsieur Lezhnev!' said Darya Mikhaylovna. 'Do sit down. I hear you know each other,' she continued, indicating Rudin.

Lezhnev glanced at Rudin and smiled in an odd way.

'I know Mr Rudin,' he said, bowing slightly.

'We were together at university,' remarked Rudin under his breath and lowered his eyes.

'We have also met since,' Lezhnev said coldly.

Darya Mikhaylovna looked with some surprise at the two of them and asked Lezhnev to sit down. He sat down.

'You wanted to see me,' he began, 'about the boundary.'

'Yes, about the boundary, but I also simply wanted to see you. After all, we're close neighbours and almost related.'

'I'm very grateful to you,' rejoined Lezhnev, 'but so far as the boundary goes I've dealt with this matter with your estate manager: I agree to all his proposals.'

'I know that . . .'

'Only he told me that without seeing you personally the papers cannot be signed.'

'Yes; that's how I've arranged things. Incidentally, may I ask, are all your peasants paying quit rent?'[3]

'They are.'

'And you concern yourself personally with boundary questions? That is praiseworthy.'

Lezhnev was silent a moment.

'So here I am, then, on a private visit,' he said.

Darya Mikhaylovna gave a smile.

'I can see you are. You say it in such a tone of voice . . . You must have been most unwilling to come here.'

'I do not go anywhere,' Lezhnev retorted phlegmatically.

'Nowhere? Don't you call on Alexandra Pavlovna?'

'I have known her brother for a long time.'

'Her brother! However, I don't like forcing anyone . . . But, forgive me, Mikhaylo Mikhaylych, I am your senior in years and I can give you a piece of my mind: what's the point of your living like an anchorite? Or is it simply *my* house you don't like? Is it me you don't like?'

'I do not know you, Darya Mikhaylovna, and therefore I cannot like or dislike you. You have a splendid house; but I must tell you frankly I don't like putting myself out. I haven't got a proper evening suit, I haven't any gloves; and what is more I don't belong to your circle.'

'By birth and upbringing you belong to it, Mikhaylo Mikhaylych! *Vous êtes des nôtres.*'

'Let's leave birth and upbringing out of it, Darya Mikhaylovna! That's not it . . .'

'A man must be sociable, Mikhaylo Mikhaylych! What's the good of sitting like Diogenes in a tub?'

'Firstly, he got on very nicely in his tub; and, secondly, how do you know I don't have my own society of friends?'

Darya Mikhaylovna bit her lip.

'That's another matter! It remains for me only to regret that I haven't been counted among their number.'

'Monsieur Lezhnev,' Rudin butted in, 'would seem to be exaggerating a most praiseworthy feeling – a love of freedom.'

Lezhnev did not answer and simply looked at Rudin. A short silence ensued.

'And so, ma'am,' began Lezhnev, rising, 'I can consider our business finished and can tell your estate manager to send me the papers.'

'You can . . . although, truth to tell, you're so discourteous I ought to refuse you.'

'The redrawing of the boundary is a great deal more advantageous to you than it is to me.'

Darya Mikhaylovna gave a shrug of her shoulders.

'You won't even have some lunch with me?' she asked.

'I thank you most humbly: I never have lunch and I'm in a hurry to be home.'

Darya Mikhaylovna stood up.

'I'm not delaying you,' she said, going over to the window. 'I wouldn't dare to.'

Lezhnev began to make his bows.

'Good-bye, Monsieur Lezhnev! Forgive me for inconveniencing you.'

'It's nothing, I assure you,' responded Lezhnev and went out.

'Did you ever?' Darya Mikhaylovna asked Rudin. 'I'd heard he was eccentric; but this is past all bounds!'

'He suffers from the same sickness as Pigasov,' said Rudin, 'a desire to be original. One plays at being a Mephistopheles, the other at being a cynic. In all this there's a great deal of egoism, a great deal of self-regard and little truth, little love. It's all based on a kind of calculation: if a man puts on a mask of indifference and apathy, someone's bound to think: What a mass of talent's gone to seed in that chap! Take a closer look – and there's no talent there at all.'

'*Et de deux!*' said Darya Mikhaylovna. 'You're a terrible one for defining people's characters. One can't hide a thing from you.'

'Do you think so?' said Rudin. 'However,' he went on, 'I shouldn't really say anything about Lezhnev; I used to love him, love him like a friend . . . but later, as a result of different misunderstandings . . .'

'You quarrelled?'

'No. But we parted, and parted, it seems, forever.'

'Indeed I noticed you weren't yourself the whole time he was here . . . Still, I'm very grateful to you for this morning. I've had an extremely pleasant time. But I mustn't detain you any longer. I'm letting you go until lunchtime, while I go and look after my affairs. My secretary, you've seen him – *Constantin, c'est lui qui est mon secrétaire* – is no doubt already waiting for me. I recommend him to you: he's an excellent, utterly obliging young man and in an absolute ecstasy over you. Until our next meeting, *cher* Dmitry Nikolaich! How grateful I am to the Baron that he introduced me to you!'

And Darya Mikhaylovna stretched out her hand to Rudin. He pressed it at first, then raised it to his lips and went out into the hall and from the hall on to the terrace. On the terrace he met Natalya.

V

DARYA MIKHAYLOVNA's daughter, Natalya Alexeyevna, might
not seem attractive at a first glance. She had not yet developed
to the full, was thin, swarthy, and inclined to be a little round-
shouldered. But the features of her face were handsome and
regular, although too big for a seventeen-year-old girl. Particularly striking was her clear, smooth forehead above delicate
eyebrows which were parted, as it were, in the middle. She
spoke little, listened and watched attentively, almost fixedly,
exactly as if she wanted to absorb everything she saw and
heard. She would frequently sit quite motionless, her hands
in her lap, and become absorbed in thought; the inner work-
ings of her thoughts would then be expressed in her face . . .
a hardly noticeable smile would suddenly appear on her lips
and vanish again; the large, dark eyes would be calmly
raised . . . '*Qu'avez-vous?*' Mlle Boncourt would ask her and
start scolding her, telling her that it was not right for a young
girl to sit there in a reverie and looking *distraite*. But Natalya
was not absent-minded: on the contrary, she applied herself
to her studies, read and worked at them gladly. She could feel
profoundly and strongly, but in secret; even in childhood she
had cried little, and now she rarely even gave a sigh and only
paled a little when something upset her. Her mother considered her a well-behaved, sensible girl, calling her jokingly:
mon honnête homme de fille, but did not have too high an opinion of her intellectual capabilities. 'My Natasha is fortunately
cool in her feelings,' she would say, 'not like me, which is
so much the better. She will be happy.' Darya Mikhaylovna
was mistaken. It's a rare mother who understands her
daughter.

Natalya loved her mother and did not entirely trust her.

'You've no need to hide anything from me,' Darya Mikhaylovna once said to her, 'but if you did you'd certainly make a secret of it: you'd keep it all to yourself . . .'

Natalya looked into her mother's face and thought: 'And why shouldn't I keep things to myself?'

When Rudin met her on the terrace she was on the way with Mlle Boncourt to her room to put on a hat before going for a walk in the garden. Her morning studies were already over. Natalya was no longer treated like a little girl and Mlle Boncourt had long ago stopped giving her lessons on mythology and geography; but Natalya had each morning to read history books, travel books, and other edifying works in her presence. Darya Mikhaylovna used to choose the books as if keeping to a special system of her own. In fact she simply handed over to Natalya everything she was sent by a French bookseller from St Petersburg, with the exception, of course, of the novels of Dumas *fils* and the like.[1] These novels Darya Mikhaylovna read herself. Mlle Boncourt used to give particularly severe and disapproving looks over the top of her spectacles whenever Natalya read history books: according to the old Frenchwoman's ideas the whole of history was full of inadmissible things, although among the great heroes of antiquity she knew for some reason only about Cambyses and in recent times only Louis XIV and Napoleon, whom she couldn't stand.[2] But Natalya also read books whose very existence Mlle Boncourt did not suspect: she knew all Pushkin by heart . . .[3]

Natalya blushed slightly on meeting Rudin.

'You're off for a walk?' he asked her.

'Yes. We're going into the garden.'

'May I come with you?'

Natalya looked at Mlle Boncourt.

'*Mais certainement, monsieur, avec plaisir,*' the elderly maiden lady said hurriedly.

Rudin seized his hat and joined them on their walk.

To start with Natalya felt awkward walking beside Rudin along the same path; after a while she felt easier. He began questioning her about her studies and how she liked being in the country. She answered not without shyness, but without that reticent haste which so frequently passes for bashfulness. Her heart beat fast.

'You don't get bored in the country?' asked Rudin, giving her a sideways look.

'How can one be bored in the country? I'm very glad that we're here. I'm very happy here.'

'You're happy ... That's a great thing to be able to say. However, it's understandable: you're young.'

Rudin uttered this last word rather oddly, as if he not so much envied Natalya as pitied her for being young.

'Yes, youth!' he added. 'The whole aim of learning is to reach consciously what is given to youth for nothing.'

Natalya gave Rudin an attentive look: she did not understand him.

'I've spent the whole morning talking with your mother,' he went on. 'She is an extraordinary woman. I can understand why all our poets cherished her friendship. Do you like poetry?' he added, after pausing a moment.

'He is testing me,' thought Natalya and said:

'Yes, I'm very fond of it.'

'Poetry is the language of the gods. I'm personally very fond of verse. But poetry is not in verse alone: everything is drenched in poetry, it is all around us ... Look at these trees, at the sky – everything breathes beauty and vitality; and where there is beauty and vitality, there is also poetry.'

'Let's sit down here on a seat,' he continued. 'That's right. It seems to me that when you get used to me' (and he glanced in her face with a smile) 'we'll be friends. What do you think?'

'He's talking to me like a child,' was what Natalya was thinking and, not knowing what to say, asked him whether he intended to stay long in the country.

'The whole summer, the autumn, and perhaps the winter. I'm a man, you know, without very many means; my affairs are in a mess, and moreover I've got bored with traipsing around from place to place. It's time to have a rest.'

Natalya was astonished.

'Do you really find it's time for you to have a rest?' she asked shyly.

Rudin turned to face Natalya.

'What do you mean?'

'I mean,' she replied with a certain embarrassment, 'that others can take a rest, but you ... you should work, you should try to be useful. Who should it be if not you ...'

'I'm grateful to you for the flattering opinion,' Rudin interrupted her. 'Be useful – that's easily said!' (He passed his hand across his face.) 'Be useful!' he repeated. 'If I were even firmly convinced how I could be useful – if I even believed in my own powers – where could genuine, sympathetic spirits be found?'

And Rudin gave such a hopeless wave of the hand and bent his head so sadly that Natalya couldn't help asking herself: surely this couldn't be the man whose ecstatic speeches breathed such optimism the night before?

'However, no,' he added, suddenly shaking his leonine head of hair, 'that's nonsense and you're right. I'm grateful to you, Natalya Alexeyevna, sincerely grateful to you.' (Natalya had no idea at all what he was grateful to her for.) 'What you've just said has reminded me of my duty and shown me the way I ought to go ... Yes, I must act. I mustn't hide my talent, if I have any; I mustn't waste my powers on talk, empty, useless talk, on mere words ...'

And his words poured out like a river. He spoke beautifully, heatedly, convincingly – about the shamefulness of a faint heart and apathy, about the need to do what had to be done. He covered himself in reproaches, arguing that to expatiate beforehand on what one wanted to do was as harmful as sticking pins into ripening fruit, that it was only a pointless waste of natural powers and juices. He affirmed that there is

78

no such thing as a noble thought which did not command sympathy, that the only people who remain misunderstood are those who either do not know what they want or are not worth understanding. He spoke at length and ended by once more expressing his gratitude to Natalya Alexeyevna, and quite unexpectedly he squeezed her hand, saying: 'You beautiful, noble creature!'

This liberty astounded Mlle Boncourt who, notwithstanding her forty-year residence in Russia, understood Russian with difficulty and could only marvel at the graceful fluency and smoothness of the speech pouring from Rudin's lips. However, in her eyes he was something of a virtuoso or artiste; and of that sort of person, according to her ideas, it was impossible to demand an observance of the decencies.

She stood up and, briskly putting her dress to rights, announced to Natalya that it was time to go back to the house, more especially since *monsieur Volinsoff* (as she called Volyntsev) wanted to come to lunch.

'And there he is!' she added, glancing down one of the paths which led from the house.

In fact, Volyntsev had appeared not far away.

He approached with an irresolute step, exchanged bows with each in turn from some distance and, his face expressing sickliness as he turned to Natalya, said:

'Ah! You are out for a walk?'

'Yes,' answered Natalya. 'We are already on our way back.'

'Ah!' uttered Volyntsev. 'Well, then, let's go together.'

And they all walked towards the house.

'How is your sister's health?' Rudin inquired of Volyntsev in a particularly solicitous voice. On the previous evening he had been very courteous to him.

'My humble thanks for your inquiry. She is well. She will today be here perhaps ... You were discussing something, I think, when I arrived?'

'Yes, Natalya Alexeyevna and I were having a discussion.

She said something that had a strong effect on me . . .'

Volyntsev did not ask what this was, and they all returned to Darya Mikhaylovna's house in profound silence.

Before dinner there was another *salon*. Pigasov, however, did not come. Rudin was not on his best form; he kept on insisting that Pandalevsky should play Beethoven. Volyntsev said nothing and kept on looking down at the floor. Natalya remained beside her mother and sat absorbed in thought or her work by turns. Basistov did not take his eyes off Rudin, all the time awaiting the moment when he would say something clever. In this way three hours or so passed fairly dully. Alexandra Pavlovna did not come to dinner – and Volyntsev, as soon as everyone rose from the table, at once ordered his carriage and slipped away without saying good-bye.

He had a heavy heart. He had long loved Natalya and been trying to pluck up the courage to propose to her . . . She was kindly disposed to him, but her heart remained unaroused: he could see that plainly. He could not hope to stir more tender feelings in her and simply waited for the moment when she would become thoroughly used to him and grow close to him. What, then, could be the source of his anxiety? What change had he noted in Natalya in the last two days? Natalya had treated him exactly as she had treated him before . . .

It might be that the idea had sunk into his heart that perhaps he did not know Natalya's temperament at all, that she was much less familiar to him than he had thought, it might be that jealousy had awoken in him, that he vaguely sensed something unpleasant was about to happen . . . yet he simply found himself suffering, no matter how he tried to persuade himself otherwise.

When he entered his sister's room he found Lezhnev sitting with her.

'Why have you returned so early?' asked Alexandra Pavlovna.

'I just did! It was boring.'

'Was Rudin there?'

'He was.'

Volyntsev cast aside his cap and sat down.

Alexandra Pavlovna turned to him vivaciously.

'Please, Seryozha, help me convince this stubborn man' (she pointed at Lezhnev) 'that Rudin is unusually clever and eloquent.'

Volyntsev mumbled something.

'I don't quarrel with you over that in the least,' Lezhnev began, 'I don't doubt Mr Rudin's intellect and eloquence; I'm simply saying that I don't like him.'

'You've met him?' asked Volyntsev.

'I saw him this morning at Darya Mikhaylovna's. Now *he*'s her great panjandrum. The time will come when she'll get rid of him – the only person she'll never get rid of is Pandalevsky – but now he's got pride of place. I saw him, of course I did! He was sitting there and she was showing me to him as though she were saying: Just look, my good sir, at the eccentric types we have round here! I'm not a stud-horse, I'm not used to being shown off. I upped and left.'

'But what were you calling on her for?'

'About a boundary question. Though that's a lot of nonsense. She simply wanted to see what I looked like. You know what women are!'

'His superiority offends you – that's what it is!' Alexandra Pavlovna claimed heatedly. 'That's why you can't forgive him. But I'm sure that, apart from his mind, he also has an exceptional heart. You take a look at his eyes when he ...'

'Of honour all resplendent speaks ...' quoted Lezhnev.[4]

'You'll annoy me and I'll start crying. I'm heartily sorry I didn't go to Darya Mikhaylovna and remained with you. You're not worth it. That's enough of teasing me,' she added plaintively. 'You'd much better tell me about his youth.'

'Rudin's youth?'

'Well, yes. After all, you told me you know him well and have known him a long time.'

Lezhnev rose and walked about the room.

'Yes,' he began, 'I know him well. You want me to tell you about his youth, do you? So be it. He was born in Tambov of poor, landowning stock. His father died soon after he was born. He was left alone with his mother. She was a woman of the utmost kindliness and thought the world of him: she lived on nothing but oatmeal and used every penny she had on him. He received his education in Moscow, in the beginning at the expense of some uncle or other, later, when he had stopped being a fledgeling and had spread his wings, with the help of a certain rich prince whom he'd sucked up to ... well, forgive me, I won't ... with whom he'd become friendly. After that he entered university. At university I got to know him and struck up a very close friendship with him. One day I'll tell you what our life was like then. I can't now. Then he went abroad ...'

Lezhnev went on walking about the room; Alexandra Pavlovna followed him with her eyes.

'From abroad,' he continued, 'Rudin wrote to his mother extremely rarely and visited her only once, for about ten days ... The old woman died without him, in the arms of strangers, but right up to the moment of death she did not take her eyes off his portrait. I used to go and visit her when I was living in Tambov. She was a kind soul and enormously hospitable and always plied me with cherry jam. She loved her Mitya to distraction. Gentlemen of the Pechorin school[5] will tell you that we always love those who are themselves little capable of love; but *I* think all mothers love their children, particularly if they're absent. Then I met Rudin abroad. There a young woman from our Russian colony had attached herself to him, some blue stocking or other, no longer young and not good-looking, just as a blue stocking should be. He went around with her for quite a long time and finally discarded her ... or no, I'm wrong: it was she who discarded him. And then I discarded him. And that's all.'

Lezhnev fell silent, passed his hand across his brow and, as though exhausted, dropped into an armchair.

'You know something, Mikhaylo Mikhaylich,' began Alexandra Pavlovna, 'I see you've got a wicked tongue; really you're no better than Pigasov. I'm sure everything you've said is the truth, that you've not invented any of it, and yet you've presented everything in such an unpleasant light! The poor old woman, her devotion, her lonely death, this young woman ... What's it all for? You know you can paint the life of the best sort of person in such colours – and not adding a thing, mind you – that one could be quite horrified at it! That's also a kind of slander!'

Lezhnev stood up and again set off about the room.

'I didn't at all want to make you horrified, Alexandra Pavlovna,' he declared at length. 'I'm not a slanderer. But,' he added after a moment's thought, 'there is actually some truth in what you've said. I wasn't slandering Rudin; but – who knows – perhaps since then he has managed to change, perhaps I've been unjust to him.'

'There now, you see! ... Promise me, then, that you'll renew your acquaintance with him, get to know him really well and only then give me your final opinion of him.'

'If you wish ... But why haven't you said anything, Sergey Pavlych?'

Volyntsev shuddered and raised his head, as if he had been woken up.

'What can I say? I don't know him. Besides, I've got a headache.'

'You do look a bit pale today,' remarked Alexandra Pavlovna. 'Are you sure you're well?'

'I've got a headache,' Volyntsev repeated and went out.

Alexandra Pavlovna and Lezhnev watched him go and exchanged looks, but said nothing. What was occurring in Volyntsev's heart was no secret for either of them.

VI

MORE than two months passed. In the course of this time Rudin remained almost wholly at Darya Mikhaylovna's. She could not do without him. To tell him about herself and listen to what he had to say became a necessity for her. He had once wanted to leave on the pretext that his money had run out: she gave him five hundred roubles. He also borrowed about two hundred roubles from Volyntsev. Pigasov took to visiting Darya Mikhaylovna a good deal less frequently: Rudin oppressed him by his presence. However, this was an oppression felt not only by Pigasov.

'I do not like this know-all,' he would say. 'He has a way of expressing himself unnaturally – the spitting image of some figure from a Russian folktale, he'll say: "I" and be at a loss for words in sheer wonderment: "I did this, I did that . . ." All the time he's making use of long words. You sneeze, and he'll at once start proving to you why you sneezed and didn't cough . . . When he praises you, it's as if he were giving you promotion in the public service . . . He starts criticizing himself, covering himself in all kinds of dirt, and you think – surely, he won't dare show his face in public again. Not a bit of it! He's gay as a canary, just as if he'd taken a swig of vodka.'

Pandalevsky was wary of Rudin and cautiously made much of him. Volyntsev found his relations with him on a strange footing. Rudin called him a knight errant and lauded him to the skies; but Volyntsev could not like him and felt an involuntary impatience and vexation each time the latter set about analysing his virtues in his presence. 'Isn't he really laughing at me?' he would think, and hostility would stir in his heart. Volyntsev tried to master his feelings; but he could not help feeling envious of Rudin in his relations with Natalya. And Rudin himself, although he was always loud in his welcome for Volyntsev, although he called him 'a most gallant knight' and borrowed money from him, was scarcely all that favourably disposed to him. It would have been hard to say exactly what these two men felt when, shaking hands with each other in the manner of friends, they looked into each other's eyes . . .

Basistov continued to worship Rudin and catch every winged word he spoke. Rudin paid little attention to him. On one occasion he spent a whole morning with him, discussed with him the most important world problems and aims and aroused in him the most lively enthusiasm, only to drop him afterwards . . . Evidently it was only so much talk on his part that he was seeking pure and devoted fellow spirits. With Lezhnev, who had begun to pay visits to Darya Mikhaylovna, Rudin did not even enter into discussion and seemed to want nothing to do with him. Lezhnev also treated him coldly, but did not, to Alexandra Pavlovna's great dismay, express his final opinion of him. She doted on Rudin; but she also had faith in Lezhnev. Everyone in Darya Mikhaylovna's house was obedient to Rudin's every wish: his least want was met. The plan of the day's activities depended on him. No *partie de plaisir* was arranged without him. Yet he was not a great enthusiast for sudden jaunts and outings and took part in them, like adults in children's games, with kindly and slightly bored deference. This apart, he busied himself with everything: discussed with Darya Mikhaylovna her management of the estate, the education of the children, domestic arrangements, and generally all her affairs; listened to what she proposed, was not even put out by matters of detail, proposed changes and new ideas. Darya Mikhaylovna sang his praises – and that was all. In the actual management of affairs she stuck to the advice of her estate manager, an elderly one-eyed Ukrainian, a good-natured and cunning old rogue. 'Age be fat 'n' wise, youth be thin in size,' he used to say, calmly smirking and winking his only eye.

After Darya Mikhaylovna Rudin talked with no one as often and as long as he did with Natalya. He used secretly to give her books, divulged to her his plans and read her the first pages of projected articles and literary works. Their sense often remained inaccessible to Natalya. However, Rudin, it seemed, was not unduly worried whether she understood – so long as she listened to him. His close relations with Natalya were not entirely to Darya Mikhaylovna's taste. 'But,' she thought, 'let her chatter away with him in the country. She entertains him with her talk like a little girl. There's no great harm in it, and she'll pick up some learning in the course of it. In St Petersburg I'll soon put a stop to it all . . .'

Darya Mikhaylovna was making a mistake. It was not like a little girl that Natalya chattered with Rudin: she listened greedily to his speeches, tried to penetrate to their meaning, subjected her own thoughts and apprehensions to his judgement; and he was her mentor, her guide. For a while, only her head felt the giddy effect, but a young head cannot be giddy all by itself. How sweet were the moments that Natalya experienced when, as used to happen, seated on a small bench in the garden, in the light, transparent shade of an ash tree, Rudin would begin reading to her from Goethe's *Faust*, from Hoffman, the *Letters* of Bettina or Novalis,[1] continually stopping and explaining to her the parts that had seemed difficult for her! She spoke German badly, like practically all our Russian young ladies, but she could understand it well, while Rudin was steeped in German poetry, in the world of German Romanticism and German philosophy and drew her with him into those lands of fairytale promise. Mysterious and beautiful, they were spread out before her attentive gaze; from the pages of the book which Rudin held in his hands wonderful pictures and new, mint-bright ideas literally poured in resonant torrents into her soul, and in her heart, shaken by the noble joy of great feelings, a sacred spark of exultation was gently kindled and caught alight . . .

'Tell me, Dmitry Nikolaich,' she began saying once, seated by the window at her embroidery, 'won't you be going to St Petersburg for the winter?'

'I don't know,' Rudin replied, letting the book which he was leafing through rest on his knees. 'If I can collect the means to do so, I will.'

He spoke flaccidly: he had felt tired and he had been inactive ever since the morning.

'I'm wondering: why can't the means be found?'

Rudin shook his head.

'You're wondering!'

And he glanced significantly away to one side.

Natalya was about to say something and hesitated.

'Look,' Rudin began and pointed through the window, 'see that apple tree: it has broken down under the weight and abundance of its own fruit. That is the true emblem of genius . . .'

'It has broken down because it wasn't given any support,' said Natalya.

'I understand what you mean, Natalya Alexeyevna; but it's not so easy for a man to find it, this support.'

'It seems to me that the sympathy of others . . . in any event, isolation . . .'

Natalya became a little confused and reddened.

'And what will you do in the country in winter?' she hastily added.

'What will I do? I will finish my extended article – you know, the one about the tragic in life and art, I told you the plan of it the day before yesterday – and I'll send it to you.'

'And will you publish it?'

'No.'

'Why not? Who will you be doing it all for, then?'

'Let it be for you.'

Natalya lowered her eyes.

'It would be beyond me, Dmitry Nikolaich!'

'What is your article about, may I ask?' Basistov, who had been sitting some distance away, inquired modestly.

'About the tragic in life and art,' Rudin repeated. 'There you are, Mr Basistov will read it. However, I haven't yet completely settled the basic idea. I haven't yet sufficiently clearly elucidated for myself the tragic significance of love.'

Rudin talked readily and frequently about love. At first, at the sound of the word 'love', Mlle Boncourt had been inclined to shudder and prick up her ears, like an old cavalry charger at the sound of a trumpet, but later she became accustomed to it and would merely purse her lips and take a pinch of snuff from time to time.

'It seems to me,' Natalya remarked shyly, 'that the tragic in love is an unhappy love.'

'Not at all!' Rudin retorted. 'That's rather the comic side of love . . . The question should be put in an entirely different way . . . One should go much deeper. Love!' he went on. 'Everything is mysterious about it: how it comes, how it grows, how it goes. It may appear suddenly, sure and radiant like the day; it may smoulder for ages, like fire beneath ashes, and burst into flame in the spirit when everything is already destroyed; or it may creep surreptitiously into the heart like a snake, or it may suddenly slip away out of it . . . yes, yes, it's a question of the utmost importance. Who can love in our time? Who can dare to love?'

And Rudin became thoughtful.

'Why haven't we seen Sergey Pavlych for a long time?' he suddenly asked.

Natalya crimsoned and bent her head over her embroidery.

'I don't know,' she whispered.

'What a really splendid, really noble fellow he is!' Rudin declared, rising. 'He is one of the best examples of the real Russian gentry . . .'

Mlle Boncourt looked askance at him out of her little French eyes.

Rudin walked about the room.

'Have you noticed,' he said, turning sharply on his heels, 'that on an oak – and an oak is a strong tree – the old leaves only begin falling when the young ones have begun to break through?'

'Yes,' replied Natalya slowly, 'I have.'

'Exactly the same thing happens with an old love in a strong heart: it may already have died but it clings on; only another, a new love, can oust it.'

Natalya did not respond. 'What's that mean?' she wondered.

Rudin stopped a moment, shook back his hair and left the room.

Natalya, meanwhile, went to her own room. She sat for a long time distractedly on her bed, mulling over Rudin's last words, and suddenly pressed her hands together and started weeping bitterly. What she was weeping about – God only knows! She herself had no idea why her tears had poured out so unexpectedly. She wiped them away, but they flowed again, like water from a well-spring long since filled to overflowing.

That very same day, at Alexandra Pavlovna's, there was a conversation between her and Lezhnev about Rudin. At first he would not say a thing; but she was determined to elicit something from him.

'I see,' she said to him, 'that you dislike Dmitry Nikolaich as much as ever. I've deliberately not asked you about it until now; but now you've had time to make sure whether or not there's been any change in him, and I want to know why you still dislike him.'

'Very well, then,' replied Lezhnev with his habitual phlegm, 'if you're as impatient as all that, I will, but look, you mustn't be angry . . .'

'Oh, do get on with it, please.'

'And you've got to let me finish.'

'Certainly, certainly, but do begin.'

'Well, ma'am,' began Lezhnev, slowly lowering himself on to the sofa, 'I tell you I really do not like Rudin. He's a clever chap . . .'

'You don't say!'

'He's a remarkably clever chap, although deep down he's empty . . .'

'That's easily said!'

'Although deep down he's empty,' Lezhnev repeated. 'But that's not what's wrong – after all, we're all empty people. I don't even hold it against him that in his soul he's a despot, that's he's lazy, that he's not very well informed . . .'

Alexandra Pavlovna clasped her hands.

'Not very well informed! Rudin!' she cried.

'Not very well informed,' Lezhnev repeated in exactly the same voice. 'He has a fondness for living off people, acting a part and so on . . . That's all in the order of things. But what's bad is that he is as cold as ice.'

'He, that fiery spirit, cold!' Alexandra Pavlovna sharply interrupted.

'Yes, cold as ice, and he knows it and pretends to be fiery. What's just as bad,' Lezhnev continued, gradually warming to the subject, 'is that he's playing a dangerous game – dangerous not for him, needless to say; he wouldn't bet so much as a farthing or a hair of his head – but others would bet their souls . . .'

'About whom, about what are you talking? I don't follow you,' said Alexandra Pavlovna.

'What's bad is that he's not honest. After all, he's a clever chap: he should know the value of his own words – but he utters them as if they really cost him something . . . There's no disputing that he's eloquent; only his eloquence isn't Russian. And it's all very well, finally, for a youngster to make grand speeches, but at his age it's shameful to take such delight in the sound of his own eloquence, it's shameful to show off!'

'It seems to me, Mikhaylo Mikhaylych, that it's immaterial to the audience whether you show off or not . . .'

'Forgive me, Alexandra Pavlona, it isn't immaterial. One man'll tell me something and it'll penetrate me through and through, another'll say the same thing and even more eloquently – and I won't so much as twitch an ear. Why is that?'

'You mean *you* won't,' Alexandra Pavlovna interrupted.

'Yes, I won't,' responded Lezhnev, 'although my ears may even be on the large size. The thing is that Rudin's words remain words and will never become deeds – and in the meantime these very words can upset and ruin a young heart.'

'Who, who are you talking about, Mikhaylo Mikhaylych?'

Lezhnev stopped.

'You want to know who I'm talking about? I'm talking about Natalya Alexeyevna.'

Alexandra Pavlovna was momentarily disconcerted, but at once gave a smile.

'Goodness gracious,' she began, 'what odd ideas you always have! Natalya's still a child; and anyhow, even if there was something in it, do you think that Darya Mikhaylovna . . .'

'In the first place, Darya Mikhaylovna is an egoist and lives only for herself; and, in the second place, she's so sure of her ability to bring up children that it wouldn't so much as enter her head to trouble herself about them. Fie! Impossible! a wave of the hand, a majestic glance – and everything's back in line. That's how she thinks, this *grande dame*, who imagines herself a patroness of the arts and an intellectual and God knows what, while in fact she's no more than an old, high-society crone. And Natalya's no child; believe me, she thinks more deeply and more often than you and I. And now this honest, passionate, ardent girl's got to come across this actor of a fellow, this coquette of a man! However, that's also in the order of things.'

'A coquette! Are you calling him a coquette?'

'Of course I am ... Well, tell me yourself, Alexandra Pavlovna, what role has he got at Darya Mikhaylovna's? Being an idol, an oracle in the household, getting involved in the domestic arrangements, in family gossip and squabbles – is that worthy of a real man?'

Alexandra Pavlovna looked with astonishment into Lezhnev's face.

'I simply don't recognize you, Mikhaylo Mikhaylych,' she said. 'You've grown red in the face, you've become excited. I can't help feeling there must be something else, something hidden ...'

'Well, well, it's as it should be! You tell a woman something out of simple conviction and she can't be content until she's thought up some superficial, irrelevant reason why you should have said that and not something else.'

Alexandra Pavlovna was angered.

'Well I never, Monsieur Lezhnev, you're beginning to persecute women no less than Mr Pigasov! But have it your way – still, no matter how perceptive you are, I find it difficult to believe that you could have understood all and everything in such a short time. I think you're mistaken. In your opinion, Rudin is some kind of Tartuffe.[2]

'The point is he's not even a Tartuffe. The real Tartuffe at least knew what he was after, but this one, with all his intellect ...'

'What is he, for heaven's sake? Do finish what you want to say, you unjust, beastly man!'

Lezhnev stood up.

'Listen, Alexandra Pavlovna,' he began, 'you're the one who's being unjust, not me. You're vexed with me for my sharp condemnation of Rudin: I've got a right to speak sharply of him! It may be that I haven't bought the right all that cheaply. I know him well: I shared lodgings with him a long time. You'll remember I promised to tell you some time or other what our life in Moscow was like then. Evidently the time's now come to do that. But will you have the patience to listen to me?'

'Go on, go on!'

'Very well, then.'

Lezhnev took to pacing slowly up and down the room, occasionally stopping and inclining his head forward.

'Perhaps you know,' he started saying, 'or perhaps you don't know that I was an orphan from an early age and by the age of seventeen I had no adult in charge of me. I lived in the house of an aunt in Moscow and did what I liked. I was a fairly empty-headed and conceited youth, fond of showing off and boasting. When I entered university I behaved like a schoolboy and was soon in a mess. I won't tell you the whole story: it isn't worth it. I lied, and I lied fairly viciously . . . The whole thing came to light, I was found out and thoroughly shamed . . . I broke down and cried like a child. It happened in the lodgings of a friend, in front of many fellow students. They all started laughing at me, all of them except one student who – more than the others, mind you – had reason to be indignant so long as I persisted and didn't confess to my lying. I don't know whether he felt sorry for me, except that he took me by the arm and led me away to his own place.'

'And that was Rudin?' asked Alexandra Pavlovna.

'No, it wasn't Rudin. It was someone . . . he's dead now . . it was someone quite out of the ordinary. His name was Pokorsky. I simply can't describe him in a few words, but once one's started talking about him one simply doesn't want to talk about anyone else. He had a lofty and pure soul and a mind such as I've never met since. Pokorsky lived in a tiny, low-ceilinged room on the mezzanine floor of an old wooden house. He was very poor and scraped by through giving lessons. There were times when he couldn't even offer a guest a cup of tea; and his only divan had sagged so much in the middle it looked like a boat. But despite these discomforts people flocked to him. Everyone loved him and he had a heart-warming attraction for people. You can't believe how delightful and enjoyable it was to sit in his wretched little room! It was there that I got to know Rudin. He had already broken his connections with his prince.'

'What was there so particular about this Pokorsky?' asked Alexandra Pavlovna.

'How can I put it? Poetry and truth – that's what attracted everyone to him. With a mind that was lucid and expansive he was still as charming and amusing as a child. I still have his bright ringing laughter in my ears, and yet at the same time he

> Burned like midnight oil
> Before the altar of good ...

That's how one half-mad and most charming poet of our group expressed himself about him.'[3]

'But how did he speak?' Alexandra Pavlovna again asked.

'He spoke well when he was in good spirits, but not astonishingly well. Rudin even in those days was twenty times more eloquent than he was.'

Lezhnev stopped his pacing and folded his arms.

'Pokorsky and Rudin bore no resemblance to each other. Rudin had a great deal more surface brilliance and sensationalism, more high-flown phrases and, I grant you, more enthusiasm. He seemed much more gifted than Pokorsky, but in fact he was a beggar by comparison. Rudin was excellent at developing an idea and he was masterley in argument; but the ideas weren't produced in his head: he took them from others, particularly from Pokorsky. To look at, Pokorsky was quiet and soft, even weak – and he loved women to distraction, liked drinking, and he wasn't one to take an insult lying down. Rudin seemed full of fire, heroism, vitality, but deep-down he was cold and even withdrawn, so long as his ego wasn't involved: in that case he'd be up in arms. He tried every way of dominating people, but he dominated them in the name of universal principles and ideas and he did in fact have a strong influence on many. True, no one was fond of him; probably I was the only one to be attracted to him. They bore his yoke ... while they surrendered to Pokorsky of their own accord. On the other hand, Rudin never refused to discuss things and argue with the first person who came along ... He hadn't read too many books but in any case a great deal more than Pokorsky and all of us; what's more, he had a systematic mind and a capacious memory – and that's the sort of thing that has an effect on young people! Give them formulae, give them conclusions, even incorrect ones, but conclusions! A completely honest man wouldn't do that. Try telling young people that you can't give them the whole truth because you don't possess it yourself ... they won't even begin to listen to you. But you also can't pull the wool over their eyes. You've got to half believe, as it were, that you're in possession of the truth ... That's why Rudin had such a strong effect on the likes of us students. You see, I told you just now that he hadn't read all that much, but he'd read books on philosophy, and his mind was so constituted that he could immediately extract from what he'd read the general principles, could grasp the root issue and then draw from it on all sides radiant, straight lines of thought and open up perspectives of the spirit. Our group consisted at that time, to tell the truth, of little boys – and poorly educated little boys at that. Philosophy, art, science, life itself – they were all so many words to us, or perhaps concepts that were alluring and beautiful, but dispersed and disunited. We weren't conscious of, had no awareness of, anything in common between these concepts, of any general world law, although we talked obscurely about it and tried to make out what it was ... Listening to Rudin we thought for the first time we'd at last grasped it, this common connection, that at last a curtain had been raised! Granted that none of what he said was his own – one couldn't ask for that! – but well-balanced orderliness was introduced into everything we knew, all the dispersed parts suddenly came together, began to take shape, grew up before our eyes like a building, all was bright with meaning, the spirit of things could be felt everywhere ... Nothing remained senseless or accidental: everything evinced rational necessity and beauty, everything acquired a meaning that was simultaneously lucid and mysterious, every individual part of life rang with a common accord, and we ourselves, with a kind of sacred worshipful awe, with a sweet quivering of our hearts, felt as if we were living vessels of eternal truth, its instruments called to accomplish something great ... Am I making you laugh?'

'Not in the least!' Alexandra Pavlovna replied gradually. 'Why do you think that? I don't understand you completely, but it doesn't make me laugh!'

'We've got a bit wiser since then, of course,' Lezhnev continued. 'It can all seem childish to us now. But I repeat, we owed Rudin a great deal in those days. Pokorsky was incomparably greater, there's no doubt of that; Pokorsky would breathe fire and strength into us, but he sometimes felt uninspired and said nothing. He was a nervy man, in poor health; yet when he spread his wings – my God, where didn't he fly to! Into the very depths, into the very azure of the heavens! But in Rudin, in this handsome and personable fellow, there was much that was trivial; he was even a bit of a gossip; he had a passion for interfering in things, giving everything his own definition and explanation. There was never any end to his bustling activity ... a true busybody politician! I speak of him as I knew him then. However, unfortunately he's not changed. Yet he's also not changed his beliefs ... in all of thirty-five years! Not everyone can say that of himself.'

'Do sit down,' said Alexandra Pavlovna. 'What are you pacing up and down the room for like a pendulum?'

'It makes me feel better,' Lezhnev replied. 'Well, having

found myself in Pokorsky's group, I must tell you, Alexandra Pavlovna, that I was completely reborn. I curbed my conceit, began asking questions, learned, rejoiced, worshipped – in short, it was like entering some kind of church. Yes indeed, when I think about our meetings, well, my God, there was much that was uplifting and affecting in them! Imagine a gathering of half-a-dozen boys, our only light one tallow candle, tea like slops and dry biscuits as old as Adam – but if only you'd heard our speeches and looked at our faces! Excitement in everyone's eyes, cheeks on fire, our hearts beating fast, and we'd talk about God, about truth, about the future of humanity, about poetry, sometimes talking nonsense, carried away by empty words, but what did that matter! ... Pokorsky would sit cross-legged, supporting his pale cheek with his hand, but his eyes would be literally alight. Rudin would stand in the middle of the room and talk, and talk splendidly, a perfect young Demosthenes declaiming to the roaring waves; the dishevelled head of the poet Subbotin would occasionally emit abrupt exclamations as if in his sleep; the forty-year-old mature student, Scheller, son of a German pastor, who had the reputation among us for being a very profound thinker on account of his eternal, utterly inviolable silence, would be silent in a particularly solemn way; even the gay Shchitov, the Aristophanes of our meetings, would fall quiet and merely make faces; two or three new boys would listen with excited pleasure ... And the night would fly away calmly and smoothly as if on wings. And then grey dawn would break and we'd go our different ways, brimful of feelings, happy, honourable, sober (we never even thought of having strong drink), with a kind of pleasant drowsiness in our souls ... I can remember how I'd walk the empty streets, full of tender feelings, and I'd even gaze in a sort of trustful way at the stars as if they'd grown closer to me and easier to understand ... Oh, it was a marvellous time then, and I don't want to believe that it's all gone in vain! And indeed it hasn't gone in vain – not even for those whom life may have trivialized later ... How many times I've come across such people, former fellow students! A man may seem to have become no more than an animal, but mention the name of Pokorsky to him and all the remnants of noble feelings will stir in his soul, just as if you'd unstoppered a forgotten scent bottle in a dark and dirty room ...'

Lezhnev stopped speaking; his usually colourless face was bright red.

'But why and when did you quarrel with Rudin?' asked Alexandra Pavlovna, gazing at Lezhnev in astonishment.

'I didn't quarrel with him; I just parted from him when I finally got to know him abroad. But I could have had a quarrel with him in Moscow. Even then he played an unkind joke on me.'

'What was it?'

'It was like this. I ... how can I put it? ... it doesn't really go with my figure ... I was always very ready to fall in love.'

'You?'

'Me. Strange, isn't it? Still, that's how things are. Well, I fell in love at that time with an extremely charming little girl ... What are you looking at me like that for? I could tell you something a great deal more surprising about myself.'

'And what is that, may I ask?'

'If you want to know – it was like this. During that Moscow time I used to make a habit of going on a nightly tryst ... with whom do you think? ... with a young limetree at the bottom of my garden. I would embrace its firm and slender trunk and imagine that I was embracing the whole of nature, and my heart would expand and be overwhelmed by a feeling that the whole of nature was actually pouring into it ... That's how I was! Yes, indeed! And perhaps you're thinking I didn't write verses? I did, and I even composed a whole drama in imitation of *Manfred*.[4] Among the cast of characters was a ghost with its breast covered in blood, and not its own blood, mind you, but the blood of humanity in general ... Yes, ma'am, that's how I was, please don't seem surprised ... But I was on the point of telling you about my love. I got to know a girl ...'

'And stopped your habit of trysting with the limetree?' asked Alexandra Pavlovna.

'I stopped that. This girl was the kindest and prettiest creature, with happy, clear eyes and a sweet voice.'

'You're good at descriptions,' remarked Alexandra Pavlovna with a smile.

'And you're a very stern critic,' rejoined Lezhnev. 'Well, ma'am, this girl lived with her aged father ... However, I won't go into details. I'll simply tell you that the girl was kindness itself – she'd everlastingly pour you three-quarters of a cupful of tea when you only asked for half a cup! ... A couple of days after my first meeting with her I was already burning with love and after a week I couldn't contain myself any longer and confessed everything to Rudin. A young man in love can hardly stop chattering about it, and I always unburdened myself to Rudin. I was then entirely under his influence, and that influence, I will say plainly, was beneficial in many respects. He was the first to take an interest in me and make something of me. I was passionately fond of Pokorsky and felt a certain awe of his spiritual purity; but I was closer to Rudin. Learning of my love he became unspeakably excited: congratulated, hugged me and instantly set about enlightening me, explaining to me the full importance of my new state. I listened open-mouthed ... Well, you know how he can talk. His words had an extraordinary effect on me. I suddenly conceived a surprising respect for myself, adopted a serious look and gave up laughing. I remember I even began walking about more carefully as if I had in my heart a bowl full of priceless liquid which I was frightened of spilling ... I was very happy, all the more so since everyone was openly respectful of me. Rudin expressed a wish to meet the object of my affections; and I'd all but insisted on introducing him.'

'Well, now I see what the matter is,' interrupted Alexandra Pavlovna. 'Rudin alienated you from the object of your affections and since then you haven't been able to forgive him . . . I'll lay a bet I'm not mistaken!'

'And you'd lose your bet, Alexandra Pavlovna: you are mistaken. Rudin did not alienate the object of my affections, and he didn't even want to, but he still destroyed my happiness, although, in the cold light of reason, I'm now prepared to thank him for doing so. But at that time I almost went out out of my mind. Rudin had no wish at all to do me any harm – quite the contrary! But because of his damned habit of pinning down every motion in life, his own as well as others, as if he were pinning down a butterfly, he set about explaining to both of us our own selves, our relationship, how we should behave, despotically forcing us to give an account of our feelings and thoughts, praising us, blaming us, even starting a correspondence with us – imagine that! Well, he finally drove us completely out of our senses! I'd hardly have married my girlfriend (I still had that much common sense), but at least we could have spent a few glorious months together, like Paul and Virginia;[5] but instead there were misunderstandings, all kinds of tensions – in other words, a lot of nonsense. It ended by Rudin coming to the conviction one fine day that, as a friend, he had the most sacred obligation to let the aged father know everything – and that's what he did.'

'No!' exclaimed Alexandra Pavlovna.

'Yes, and, mind you, he did it with my agreement – that's the remarkable thing! I can remember even now the chaos that I then carried round in my head: everything went round and round and got back to front as in a camera obscura: white seemed black, black – white, falsehood – truth, imagination – conscience . . . Oh, I'm ashamed to think of it now! Rudin –

well, he didn't falter. Trust him! He'd go on and on, through all manner of misunderstandings and complications, to and fro, to and fro, like a swallow over a pond.'

'And so you said good-bye to your sweet maiden?' asked Alexandra Pavlovna, naïvely inclining her head to one side and raising her eyebrows.

'I said good-bye . . . and did it badly, humiliatingly, awkwardly, publicly, and unnecessarily publicly . . . I was in tears and she was in tears and the devil knows what happened . . . a Gordian knot had been tied and it had to be cut with one blow, and that really hurt! However, everything's for the best in this world. She got married to a good man and is now flourishing . . .'

'Confess, though, that you still couldn't forgive Rudin . . .' Alexandra Pavlovna began.

'What a thing to say!' Lezhnev interrupted. 'I cried like a child when I saw him off for abroad. However, truth to tell, a seed of doubt had already been sown in my heart even then. And when I met him later, abroad . . . well, I'd already matured . . . I then saw Rudin in his real light.'

'What exactly did you find in him?'

'Everything I told you about an hour ago. Still, enough of that. Perhaps it'll all work out satisfactorily. I only wanted to prove to you that if I judge him severely it's not because I don't know him . . . So far as Natalya Alexeyevna is concerned, I won't waste needless words; but just you look at your brother.'

'My brother! Why?'

'Just look at him. Don't you notice anything?'

Alexandra Pavlovna lowered her gaze.

'You're right,' she said softly, 'exactly . . . my brother . . . for some time I've not been able to make him out . . . But surely you're not thinking . . .'

'Quiet! I think he's coming,' Lezhnev uttered in a whisper. 'But Natalya's no child, believe me, though unfortunately she's as inexperienced as a child. You wait and see, that little girl will surprise us all.'

'In what way?'

'In this way ... You know, don't you, that it is precisely little girls like that who drown themselves, take poison, and so on? You shouldn't look on her as such a quiet little thing: there are strong passions lurking in her and a character – ah, a real character!'

'Well, now I think you're rhapsodizing. To a phlegmatic man like you even I would seem a volcano.'

'Now, that's not true!' said Lezhnev with a smile. 'And so far as character goes, you haven't any character at all, thank God!'

'Why such insolence?'

'That – insolence? That's the greatest compliment, believe me . . .'

Volyntsev entered and looked suspiciously at Lezhnev and his sister. He had grown thin lately. They started talking to him, but he scarcely smiled at their jokes and looked, as Pigasov had once said of him, like a melancholy hare. However, there's probably not a man on this earth who, at least once in his life, hasn't looked worse. Volyntsev felt that Natalya was slipping away from him and that, along with her, the earth was also slipping from under his feet.

THE next day was a Sunday and Natalya got up late. The previous day she had been very taciturn right up to the evening, she had been secretly ashamed of her tears and she had slept very badly. Sitting, half-dressed, in front of her little piano, she either struck barely audible chords, so as not to wake up Mlle Boncourt, or she rested her forehead on the cold keys and remained still for long periods. She was thinking – not about Rudin but about something he had said, and she sank into this thought of hers. Occasionally the image of Volyntsev came to mind. She knew that he loved her. But her thoughts moved away from him at once . . . She felt a strange excitement. She dressed hurriedly that morning, went downstairs and having greeted her mother seized an appropriate opportunity and went out alone into the garden . . .

The day was hot and bright, a day of radiant sunlight despite intermittent showers. Low smoky clouds sailed smoothly across a clear sky without hiding the sun, and from time to time shed onto the fields plentiful downpours of sudden and momentary rainfall. The large glittering raindrops fell briskly with a kind of dry rustling like diamonds; the sunlight played through their delicate network; the grass, so recently stirred by the wind, made not a movement as it seemingly drank up the moisture; the trees under the drenching set up a languid trembling in all their leaves; the birds went on singing ceaselessly, and it was a delight to hear talkative chirruping in the fresh hiss and pitter-patter of the passing rain. The dusty roads smoked and became slightly mottled under the sharp blows of frequent gusts of rain. But then the cloud passed, a light breeze sprang up, the grass began to flow with emerald and gold . . . Clinging moistly to each other, the leaves of the trees began to let the sunlight shine through ... A heady fragrance rose on all sides ...

The sky had almost completely cleared when Natalya went into the garden. It breathed freshness and tranquillity, that gentle and happy tranquillity to which the heart of man responds with a sweetly oppressive stirring of secret sympathy and indefinable longings ...

Natalya walked beside the pond along a long avenue of silvery poplars; suddenly Rudin rose up before her as if he had come out of the ground.

She was startled. He looked into her face.

'Are you alone?' he asked.

'Yes, I'm alone,' Natalya answered. 'But I only came out for a moment. I ought to be going back to the house.'

'I'll walk with you.'

And he walked along beside her.

'Why are you looking sad?' he inquired softly.

'Me? ... I'd wanted to mention to you that you seemed in low spirits.'

'Perhaps ... I'm like that. It's more excusable in my case than in yours.'

'Why? Do you think I've got nothing to be sad about?'

'At your age one should be enjoying life.'

Natalya took several paces in silence.

'Dmitry Nikolayevich!' she declared.

'What?'

'You remember ... the comparison which you made yesterday ... remember – about the oak.'

'Er – yes, I remember. What of it?'

Natalya glanced surreptitiously at Rudin.

'Why did you ... What did you mean by that comparison?'

Rudin inclined his head to one side and stared into the distance.

'Natalya Alexeyevna!' he began, with his customary restrained and meaningful look which always made a listener think that Rudin was not uttering a tenth part of all that crowded into his soul, 'Natalya Alexeyevna, you'll have noticed I speak little about my past. There are certain heartstrings which I do not touch at all. My heart . . . Who has any need to know what has taken place within it? I have always deemed it a sacrilege to make an exhibition of such things. But with you I am utterly candid: you inspire my confidence . . . I can't hide from you that I have loved and suffered like the next man . . . When and how? That's not worth mentioning; but my heart has endured many joys and many sorrows . . .'

Rudin was silent a moment.

'What I said to you yesterday,' he went on, 'is perhaps to some extent applicable to me, to my present state. But here again this is not worth mentioning. This side of life has already vanished for me. It remains for me now to travel a hot and dusty road, from post-station to post-station, in a ramshackle cart . . . When I shall reach my destination, or whether I'll reach it, God alone knows . . . Let's talk about you instead.'

'Can you really mean, Dmitry Nikolayevich,' Natalya interrupted him, 'that you expect nothing from life?'

'Oh, no! I expect much, but not for myself . . . I shall never abandon active work, the bliss of activity, but I have already rejected personal enjoyment. My hopes and my dreams, on the one hand – and my personal happiness, on the other – have nothing in common. Love' (at this he shrugged his shoulders) 'love is not for me; I . . . do not deserve it; a woman has the right to demand everything of a man, but I am no longer capable of surrendering myself entirely. As for being liked – that's for young men: I'm too old. Why should I turn other people's heads? God grant I keep my own firmly on my shoulders!'

'I understand,' Natalya murmured, 'that a man who strives after a great aim mustn't think about himself; but is a woman in no position to know the value of such a man? On the contrary, I think a woman would sooner turn away from an egoist ... All young people – these young men you mention, they're all egoists, they're all only concerned with themselves, even when they're in love. Believe me, a woman is not only capable of understanding self-sacrifice; she knows how to sacrifice herself.'

A light crimson had spread over Natalya's cheeks, and her eyes had begun to shine. Before knowing Rudin she would never have uttered such a long speech, or uttered it so heatedly.

'You've frequently heard my opinion of the vocation of women,' rejoined Rudin with a condescending smile. 'You know it's my opinion that Joan of Arc was alone able to save France ... But that's not the point. I wanted to talk about you. You are on the threshold of life ... A discussion of your future would be both delightful and not unfruitful ... Listen: you know I'm your friend; I take an almost parental interest in you ... And so I hope you won't find my question immodest: tell me, is your heart so far completely unaroused?'

Natalya blushed crimson and said nothing. Rudin stopped in his walking, and she stopped.

'You're not angry with me, are you?' he asked.

'No,' she said. 'But I hadn't in the least expected ...'

'However,' he went on, 'you don't have to answer me. I already know your secret.'

Natalya glanced at him almost in fright.

'Yes ... yes, I know who you're fond of. And I must say you couldn't make a better choice. He's an excellent chap; he will know how to appreciate you; he's not been jaded by life – his is a simple and lucid soul ... and he'll make you happy.'

'Who are you talking about, Dmitry Nikolaich?'

'As if you don't understand who I'm talking about! Naturally about Volyntsev. What about that? It's true, isn't it?'

Natalya turned slightly away from Rudin. She was at her wits' end.

'He loves you, doesn't he? After all, he can't take his eyes off you, follows your every movement; and, in the end, can one ever hide one's love? And you're well disposed towards him, aren't you? So far as I can see, your mother also likes him ... Your choice ...'

'Dmitry Nikolaich!' Natalya interrupted him, in her embarrassment stretching out a hand to a nearby bush, 'I feel, I really do feel such awkwardness in talking about it, but I assure you ... you're wrong ...'

'I'm wrong?' Rudin repeated. 'I don't think so ... I haven't known you long, but I already know you well. What's the change which I see in you, which I see quite clearly – what's it mean? You're not the same, are you, as when I found you some six weeks ago? ... No, Natalya Alexeyevna, your heart is restless.'

'Perhaps,' Natalya answered scarcely audibly, 'but you're still mistaken.'

'How can I be?' asked Rudin.

'Go away, don't ask me any more questions!' Natalya exclaimed and set off with brisk steps towards the house.

She found herself frightened of everything she felt suddenly within her.

Rudin caught up with her and stopped her.

'Natalya Alexeyevna!' he began. 'Our talk can't end this way; it's too important to me ... What am I to understand you to mean?'

'Go away!' Natalya repeated.

'Natalya Alexeyevna, for God's sake!'

Rudin's face showed his agitation. He had grown pale.

'You understand everything, you ought to understand me as well!' cried Natalya, tearing her hand from his and walking away without looking back.

'Just one word, please!' Rudin shouted after her.

She stopped, but she did not turn round.

'You were asking me what I meant by yesterday's comparison. You must know I haven't any wish to deceive you. I was talking about myself, about my past – and about you.'

'In what way – about me?'

'Yes, it was about you; I repeat, I don't have any wish to deceive you ... You know now what the feeling was, what the new feeling was, which I was talking about just a moment ago ... Until today I'd never been able to decide ...'

Natalya suddenly covered her face with her hands and ran off towards the house.

She was so shaken by the unexpected climax to the talk with Rudin that she did not even notice Volyntsev, past whom she ran. He was standing motionless, leaning back against a tree. A quarter of an hour earlier he had arrived at Darya Mikhaylovna's and found her in the drawing-room, had exchanged a couple of words, inconspicuously left, and set off to look for Natalya. Guided by a sixth sense which those in love possess, had gone straight into the garden and encountered her and Rudin at the very moment when she had torn her hand from his. For Volyntsev everything seemed to go dark. Following Natalya with his eyes, he left the tree and took a couple of steps, not knowing where or why. Rudin caught sight of him when he came level with him. Both men looked each other in the eyes, bowed and went their way in silence.

'That's not the end of it,' both thought.

Volyntsev walked to the very end of the garden. He felt sick and miserable; there was a lead weight on his heart, and he felt his blood rise from time to time in anger. There was again a sprinkling of rain. Rudin returned to his own room. He was also disquieted: his thoughts were in a whirl. The unexpected, trustful contact of a young, honourable soul is enough to confuse anyone.

At dinner everything went rather badly. Natalya, white-faced, could scarcely remain in her place and never raised her eyes. Volyntsev sat, as usual, beside her and from time to time tried to make conversation with her. It so happened that

Pigasov was dining that day at Darya Mikhaylovna's. He talked more than anyone else at table. Among other things he began to argue that people, like dogs, can be divided into bob-tailed and long-tailed. 'People can be bob-tailed,' he said, 'both from birth and through their own fault. The bob-tailed are badly off: they don't succeed in anything, they have no self-confidence. But the man who has a long, fluffy tail is a happy man. He can be both worse and weaker than your bob-tailed type, but the point is he's sure of himself; he swishes his tail about and everyone's full of admiration. And what's surprising is: a tail's a completely useless part of the body, wouldn't you agree? What's a tail good for? Still, everyone judges your merits by your tail. I,' he added with a sigh, 'belong in the bob-tailed category, and what's so annoying is that I was the one who cut off my own tail.'

'What you mean to say,' remarked Rudin casually, 'is surely what La Rochefoucauld[1] said long before you: Be sure of yourself and others will believe in you. I can't see why you should bring tails into this.'

'Please allow a man,' said Volyntsev sharply, and his eyes were burning, 'to express himself as he wishes. Talk about despotism . . . In my view, nothing is worse than the despotism of so-called clever people. The devil take them!'

Everyone was stunned by Volyntsev's outburst and fell silent. Rudin tried to look him in the eye but could not withstand his look, turned away, smiled, and did not open his mouth.

'Aha! So you're one of the bob-tailed too!' thought Pigasov; while Natalya almost died of fright. Darya Mikhaylovna looked long and perplexedly at Volyntsev and was finally the first to start talking; she began a story about an unusual dog belonging to a friend of hers, the Minister of —

Volyntsev left soon after dinner. Taking his leave of Natalya, he could not restrain himself longer and said:

'Why are you so embarrassed, just as if you were to blame? You simply can't be to blame, not in anyone's eyes!'

Natalya did not grasp what he said and simply watched him go. Before tea was served Rudin went up to her and, bending over the table, as if sorting through some newspapers, whispered:

'It's all like a bad dream, isn't it? I must see you alone . . . if only for a moment.' He turned to Mlle Boncourt. 'Look,' he said to her, 'here's the feuilleton you were looking for,' and again leaning towards Natalya he added in a whisper: 'Try and be near the terrace about ten o'clock, in the lilac arbour; I'll be waiting for you . . .'

Pigasov was the hero of the evening. Rudin abandoned the field of battle to him. He amused Darya Mikhaylovna a great deal. He began by telling a story about a neighbour of his who, after thirty years of henpecking from his wife, had become such an old woman that, crossing a small patch of marshy ground in Pigasov's presence, he'd put his hand behind him and lifted up his coat-tails in the same way women lift up their skirts. Afterwards he talked of another landowner who'd started by being a freemason, had become a melancholic, and then wanted to be a banker.

'What was it like being a freemason, Filipp Stepanych?' Pigasov had asked him.

'Nothing to it: I just never used to cut the nails on my little fingers.'[2]

But Darya Mikhaylovna laughed most of all when Pigasov started passing remarks about love and insisting that even he had caused sighs to rise in female bosoms and that one passionate German lady had even called him her 'tasty little Afrikan chickadee and squawker'. Darya Mikhaylovna laughed, but Pigasov was telling no lie: he had a perfect right to boast of his conquests. He asserted that nothing could be easier than to make a woman love you: just go on repeating to her ten days in a row how heavenly was the sound from her lips, what bliss it was to gaze into her eyes, and that all other women by comparison were so much rubbish, and on the eleventh day she'd also say how heavenly was the sound from her lips, what bliss it was to gaze into her eyes, and be in love with you. Anything's possible on this earth. Who knows? perhaps Pigasov was right.

At half past nine Rudin was already in the arbour. In the distant and pale depths of the sky small stars were just beginning to twinkle; in the west the sky was still crimson – and the horizon there seemed clearer and purer; a half-moon gleamed like gold through the black network of a weeping birch. Other trees either stood there like sombre giants, with thousands of glimmers showing through them like so many eyes, or flowed together into solid dark masses. Not a leaf stirred; the upper branches of the lilacs and acacias seemed to be listening to something and holding themselves taut in the warm air. The house loomed darkly nearby; its long lighted windows formed splashes of reddish light. The evening was calm and peaceful; but it was as if the silence were filled by a longdrawn, passionate sigh.

Rudin stood with his arms folded and listened intently. His heart beat powerfully and he found himself holding his breath. At last he heard light, hurried footsteps and Natalya entered the arbour.

Rudin dashed towards her and seized her by the hands. They were cold as ice.

'Natalya Alexeyevna,' he began in a tremulous whisper, 'I had to see you ... I couldn't wait until tomorrow. I've got to tell you something I never suspected and didn't even know this morning: I love you.'

Natalya's hands shook faintly in his hands.

'I love you,' he repeated, 'and how could I have deceived myself so long, how didn't I guess long ago that I loved you! ... But you? Tell me, Natalya Alexeyevna, you? ...'

Natalya could scarcely draw breath.

'You can see I've come here,' she said eventually.

'But tell me, do you love me?'

'I think so . . . yes . . .' she whispered.

Rudin squeezed her hands still more firmly and wanted to draw her to him.

Natalya quickly glanced behind her.

'Let me go, I'm frightened – I think someone's overheard us . . . For heaven's sake be careful. Volyntsev's guessed.'

'God be with him! You saw how I didn't answer him to-day . . . Ah, Natalya Alexeyevna, how happy I am! Now nothing can come between us!'

Natalya glanced into his eyes.

'Let me go,' she whispered, 'it's time.'

'One moment . . .' Rudin began.

'No, let me go, let me go . . .'

'You're not frightened of me, are you?'

'No, but it's time to go . . .'

'Then at least say it again . . .'

'You say you're happy?' asked Natalya.

'Me? There's not a happier man in the world than me! You don't doubt that, do you?'

Natalya raised her head. Her pale face was beautiful, and in the mysterious twilight of the arbour, in the weak illumination of the nocturnal moon, it glowed with nobility, youthfulness, and excitement.

'You must know,' she said, 'I'll be yours.'

'Oh, my God!' exclaimed Rudin.

But Natalya leaned back from him and left. Rudin stood there for a little while and then walked slowly out of the arbour. The moonlight clearly lit up his face; a smile wandered about his lips.

'I'm happy,' he pronounced to himself in a low voice. 'Yes, I really am happy,' he repeated, as if trying to convince himself.

He straightened himself, shook back his hair, and walked

briskly into the garden, gesturing gaily to right and left.

But meanwhile in the lilac arbour the bushes were quietly parted and Pandalevsky appeared. He looked cautiously round, shook his head, pursed his lips, said significantly: 'So that's it. Darya Mikhaylovna'll have to know about this . . .' and vanished.

VIII

AFTER returning home, Volyntsev was so despondent and sombre, responded to his sister's questions so unwillingly, and was so quick to lock himself away in his study, that she decided to send someone off to fetch Lezhnev. She always turned to him in all difficult situations. Lezhnev sent word that he would be coming the next day.

Volyntsev was no more light-hearted by morning. After drinking his tea he had intended to set off to inspect the work of the estate, but he stayed at home, lay down on a divan, and set about reading, which was not a frequent occurrence in his life. Volyntsev felt no strong attraction for literature and was simply terrified of poetry. 'It's as much nonsense as poetry,' he was fond of saying and, in demonstration of his words, would quote the following lines by the poet Aybulat:[1]

> And to the end of plaintive days
> No proud experience, no mind
> Will with its hand compress and graze
> Blood-stained forget-me-nots of life.

Alexandra Pavlovna gave her brother alarmed looks, but did not disturb him with questions. A carriage drove up to the front door. 'Well,' she thought, 'thank God, it's Lezhnev ...' A servant entered and announced the arrival of Rudin.

Volyntsev threw his book on the floor and looked up.

'Who's come?' he asked.

'Rudin, Dmitry Nikolaich,' the servant repeated.

Volyntsev stood up.

'Ask him in,' he muttered. 'But you, my dear,' he added, turning to Alexandra Pavlovna, 'must leave us alone.'

'What on earth for?' she began.

'I know why,' he interrupted her shortly. 'I ask you to leave.'

Rudin entered. Volyntsev bowed coldly to him, standing in the middle of the room, and did not offer him his hand.

'You hadn't expected me, admit it,' Rudin began and placed his hat on the window-sill.

His lips were trembling slightly. He felt awkward; but he attempted to hide his confusion.

'Quite true – I hadn't expected you,' Volyntsev replied. 'After yesterday I would sooner have expected someone with a – with a message from you.'

'I know what you mean,' Rudin murmured, sitting down, 'and I'm very glad of your frankness. It's much better that way. I came to you as to an honourable man.'

'Can't we dispense with the compliments?' remarked Volyntsev.

'I want to explain to you why I've come.'

'We know each other: why shouldn't you come and see me? In any case this isn't the first time you've deigned to visit me.'

'I came to you as one honourable man to another,' repeated Rudin, 'and I now want to submit my case to your judgement . . . I trust you completely . . .'

'What is it all about, then?' asked Volyntsev, who remained standing in his former position and glared morosely at Rudin, occasionally pulling the ends of his moustache.

'Permit me to explain . . . I came in order to clear things up, naturally; but that can't be done all at once.'

'Why not?'

'A third person is involved . . .'

'What third person?'

'Sergey Pavlych, you know what I mean.'

'Dmitry Nikolaich, I haven't the slightest idea what you mean.'

'As you wish . . .'

'I wish you'd speak plainly!' Volyntsev broke in.

He was beginning to lose his temper in real earnest.

Rudin frowned.

'Very well ... we're alone ... I must tell you – besides, you've no doubt already guessed' (Volyntsev impatiently shrugged his shoulders) '... I must tell you that I love Natalya Alexeyevna and have the right to suppose that she also loves me.'

Volyntsev went pale, but instead of answering walked over to the window and stood with his back to the room.

'You understand, Sergey Pavlych,' Rudin went on, 'that if I weren't sure ...'

'Of course!' Volyntsev briskly interrupted, 'I don't doubt in the least ... Splendid! Here's to you! I'm just staggered at what the devil made you think of coming to me with this news of yours ... What's it got to do with me? Why should it concern me whom you love or who loves you? I simply can't understand it.'

Volyntsev continued to stare out of the window. His voice sounded hollow.

Rudin stood up.

'I will tell you, Sergey Pavlych, why I decided to come to you and why I didn't consider I even had the right to hide from you our ... our mutual disposition. I have too deep a respect for you – that's why I came; I didn't want ... neither of us wanted to act out a comedy in front of you. Your feeling for Natalya Alexeyevna was known to me ... Believe me, I know what I'm worth: I know how unworthy I am to take your place in her heart; but if this has been destined to happen, would it have been better to cheat and deceive and pretend? Would it have been better to submit to misunderstandings or even the possibility of a scene like the one at dinner yesterday? Sergey Pavlych, tell me.'

Volyntsev folded his arms in front of him as if forcibly holding back his feelings.

'Sergey Pavlych!' Rudin continued, 'I feel I've annoyed you ... but try and understand us ... try and understand we didn't have any other way of showing you our respect, of showing you that we know how to appreciate your directness and nobility of soul. Frankness, complete frankness would have been inappropriate with someone else, but with you it becomes an obligation. It's nice for us to think that our secret is in your hands . . .'

Volyntsev broke into forced laughter.

'Thanks for entrusting me with it!' he exclaimed, 'although, I ask you to take note, I wanted neither to know your secret nor to entrust you with mine, but you're treating it anyhow as your own property. But of course you're speaking for both of you. I take it I can presume that Natalya Alexeyevna knows about your visit and its object?'

Rudin appeared a little embarrassed.

'No, I didn't inform Natalya Alexeyevna of my intentions; but I know she shares my way of thinking.'

'Quite splendid,' said Volyntsev after a short silence, drumming his fingers against the glass, 'although I must admit it would've been a lot better if you'd respected me a little less. Truth to tell, I don't care a damn for your respect; but exactly what is it you want of me?'

'I don't want anything . . . or no! I want one thing: I want you not to think of me as cunning and underhand, I want you to understand me . . . I hope you have no reason now to doubt my sincerity . . . I would like us, Sergey Pavlych, to part as friends . . . that you would offer me your hand as you used to . . .'

And Rudin went up to Volyntsev.

'Forgive me, my dear sir,' said Volyntsev, turning round and stepping back a pace, 'I'm prepared to grant full justice to your intentions – they're all quite splendid, no doubt even exalted, but we're simple people, we're used to plain fare, we're not in a condition to follow the flight of such great minds as yours . . . What to you seems sincere, to us seems impertinent and immodest . . . What for you is simple and clear is confused and obscure to us ... You boast of things we're used to hiding: how on earth can we understand you! Forgive me, I can neither consider you my friend, nor will I offer you my hand ... Perhaps that's not profound; but then I'm not profound.'

Rudin took his hat from the window-sill.

'Sergey Pavlych!' he said sadly, 'good-bye. I've been deceived in my expectations. My visit is really rather strange, but I had hoped that you ...' (Volyntsev made an impatient gesture.) 'Forgive me, I shan't say anything more about it. Having duly considered it all, I see you're right and couldn't have behaved otherwise. Good-bye and allow me at least this once, this last time, to assure you of the purity of my intentions ... I can rely on your modesty ...'

'This is too much!' exclaimed Volyntsev, shaking with rage. 'I didn't seek your trust in the very least, and you have no right at all to count on my modesty!'

Rudin was on the point of speaking but simply spread his arms wide, bowed, and went out, while Volyntsev threw himself on to the divan and turned his face to the wall.

'May I come in?' asked Alexandra Pavlovna's voice beyond the door.

Volyntsev did not answer immediately and covertly passed his hand across his face.

'No, my dear,' he said in a slightly changed voice, 'wait a bit longer.'

Half an hour later Alexandra Pavlovna again approached the door.

'Mikhaylo Mikhaylych has come,' she said. 'Would you like to see him?'

'I would,' answered Volyntsev. 'Send him in here.'

Lezhnev entered.

'What – aren't you well?' he asked, taking a seat in the armchair next to the divan.

Volyntsev raised himself, leaned on one elbow, gazed very

long into his friend's face and then gave him a word-for-word account of his entire conversation with Rudin. He had never until that moment so much as hinted to Lezhnev of his feelings for Natalya, although he had guessed they were no secret to him.

'Well, my dear chap, you've astonished me,' declared Lezhnev as soon as Volyntsev had finished. 'I'd come to expect a good many eccentricities from him, but this . . . Still, I can recognize him even in this.'

'You don't say!' said an excited Volyntsev. 'It's a bloody liberty! I almost threw him through the window! Did he want to come and show off in front of me, or did he get cold feet? What was it all for? How can one make up one's mind to go and see someone . . .'

Volyntsev put his hands behind his head and fell silent.

'No, my dear chap, it's not that,' Lezhnev retorted calmly. 'You won't believe me, but he did it with the best of intentions. Really and truly . . . It was to be both noble and candid, can't you see? and, well, there was an opportunity of talking, of giving vent to a little eloquence; and that's what his type needs, they can't live without it . . . Oh, his tongue's his worst enemy . . . Well, of course, it also serves him well enough.'

'With what solemn self-importance he came in and spoke, you simply can't imagine!'

'Well, of course that's essential. He buttons up his jacket just as if he's fulfilling a sacred obligation. I would deposit him on an uninhabited island and then watch to see how he got on there. The way he goes on about the simple life!'

'But tell me, my dear fellow, for God's sake,' asked Volyntsev, 'what is it – is it philosophy?'

'How can I answer? On the one hand, it is, granted, precisely that – philosophy, but on the other hand it's not that at all. It's wrong to lump a whole heap of nonsense together and call it philosophy.'

Volyntsev looked at him.

'Perhaps he was lying, what do you think?'

'No, my boy, he wasn't lying. However, do you know what? We've discussed this enough. Let's light up our pipes, my dear chap, and ask Alexandra Pavlovna in ... In her presence it's easier both to talk and to keep quiet. She'll pour tea for us.'

'Splendid,' replied Volyntsev. 'Come in, my dear,' he called.

Alexandra Pavlovna came in. He seized her hand and pressed it firmly to his lips.

Rudin returned home in a confused and unusual state of spirits. He was vexed with himself and blamed himself for the unforgivable rashness and childishness of his behaviour. It's not for nothing that someone has said: There's no harder thing in the world than being aware of your own recent stupidity.

Remorse gnawed at Rudin.

'What the devil got into me,' he muttered through his teeth, 'to go calling on that landowner like that! The idea came to me, that's all! Just to invite insults!'

But meanwhile in Darya Mikhaylovna's house something unusual had been happening. The mistress of the house did not put in an appearance the entire morning and was not at dinner: she had a headache, according to Pandalevsky, who was the only person allowed to see her. Rudin also saw almost nothing of Natalya: she was sitting in her room with Mlle Boncourt. Meeting him briefly in the dining-room, she gave him such a sad look that his heart missed a beat. Her face had changed just as if a misfortune had overtaken her since the previous day. A melancholy awareness of vague forebodings began to trouble Rudin. In order to distract himself somehow or other, he occupied himself with Basistov, had a long conversation with him and discovered in him a young man of ardent and vivacious mind, with the loftiest of hopes and an as yet untrammelled capacity for belief. Towards evening Darya Mikhaylovna appeared for a couple of hours in the drawing-room. She was polite to Rudin, but kept herself at a distance and laughed and frowned by turns, talked through her nose and for the greater part in hints ... in fact she literally exuded an air of courtly bitchiness. Of late she had cooled a little in her attitude to Rudin. 'What's all the mystery?' he wondered, looking askance at her small tilted head.

He did not have to wait long for the mystery to be explained. Returning around midnight to his room, he went along a dark corridor. Suddenly someone stuck a note into his hand. He looked round: a girl – Natalya's maid, he thought – was hurrying away from him. He went to his own room, despatched his manservant, unfolded the note, and read the following lines written in Natalya's hand:

Come tomorrow between six and seven in the morning, not later, to Avdyukhin pond, beyond the oak wood. No other time is possible. It will be our last meeting, and everything will be finished, if ... Please come. We must decide ...

P.S. If I don't come, it means we won't see each other again. In that case I'll let you know ...

Rudin became thoughtful, twisted the note in his hands, placed it under his pillow, undressed, and lay down, but did not fall asleep at once and slept only lightly, awaking before it was five.

IX

AVDYUKHIN pond, which Natalya had named as their meeting-place, had long since ceased to be a pond. Some thirty years ago the dam which made it had been breached and ever since it had been left derelict. Only by noticing the smooth, flat bottom of the gully, at one time covered by a rich silt, and by noting the remains of the dam could one have guessed that there had ever been a pond here at all. At one time there had also been a house. It had vanished long ago. Two enormous pines were the only reminder of it; the wind eternally murmured and howled morosely in their high, sparse branches. Among the local peasantry there circulated mysterious legends about some awful crime which supposedly had been committed under them; it was also said that not one of them would fall without causing someone's death; that there had been a third pine which was blown down in a storm and had crushed a girl beneath it. The entire area round the old pond was considered unclean; empty and bare always, but godforsaken and sombre even on a sunny day, it seemed even darker and more abandoned through being so close to the barren oak wood which had long since died and dried up. Grey skeletons of massive trees towered here and there like mournful spectres over the low bushy undergrowth. It made the flesh creep to look at them, as if they were evil old men who had gathered together to plan some wickedness. A narrow, infrequently used track wound its way past it. Without having a special reason no one walked past Avdyukhin pond. Natalya had deliberately chosen this isolated spot. It was no more than a third of a mile from Darya Mikhaylovna's house.

The sun was already long risen when Rudin reached the pond; but it was not a cheerful morning. Massed milk-white clouds covered the entire sky; the wind drove them briskly, whistling and moaning. Rudin began walking up and down the dam that was covered with clinging burdock and blackened nettles. He was not calm. These meetings and new feelings preoccupied him, but they also excited him, particularly after yesterday's note. He saw that the denouement was approaching and was inwardly smitten, although nobody would have thought so by looking at the intent determination with which he went on folding and unfolding his arms and gazing around him. It was not for nothing that Pigasov had once compared him to a little Chinese idol whose head was always bobbing up. But with the aid only of his head, no matter how well endowed, a man would find it difficult to know even what was going on in himself ... Rudin, intelligent, perspicacious Rudin, was not in any condition to say truthfully whether he loved Natalya, whether he was suffering or would suffer when he parted from her. Why then, without pretending to be a Lovelace[1] – we must do him that much justice – did he deliberately turn the poor girl's head? Why did he wait for her with secret anxiety? There is only one answer: no one is as easily carried away by his emotions as a dispassionate man.

He paced up and down the dam while Natalya rushed to him straight across the fields, through the wet grass.

'Mistress! Mistress! you'll get your feet all wet,' her maid Masha was saying to her, hardly keeping up with her.

Natalya paid no attention to her and ran on without a glance back.

'Oh, if only they haven't seen us!' Masha was repeating over and over. 'It's simply a wonder how we got out of the house. If only mam'selle hasn't woken up ... It's a good thing it's not far ... Ah, there he is, waiting for us,' she added, suddenly catching sight of the lordly figure of Rudin standing picturesquely on the dam. 'Only there's not much sense in 'im being up there, he ought to go down into the gully.'

Natalya stopped.

'Wait here, Masha, by the pines,' she murmured and went down towards the pond.

Rudin approached her and stopped in amazement. He had never seen such an expression before on her face. Her eyebrows were drawn tightly together, her lips were tight shut, and her eyes looked directly and sternly in front of her.

'Dmitry Nikolaich,' she began, 'we have no time to waste. I've got only five minutes. I must tell you that my mother knows everything. Mr Pandalevsky saw us the day before yesterday and told her about our meeting. He was always spying for my mother. She sent for me yesterday.'

'My God!' cried Rudin. 'This is awful! What did your mother have to say?'

'She wasn't angry with me, she didn't scold me, she simply told me off for being frivolous.'

'Is that all?'

'Yes. And she announced she'd rather agree to see me dead than your wife.'

'Did she really say that?'

'Yes. And she added that you yourself hadn't the least wish to marry me, that you'd simply been amusing yourself with me, out of boredom, and that she hadn't expected this of you; that she, however, was the one to blame for letting me see you so often ... that she puts her trust in my good sense, that I'd been a great surprise to her ... oh, I don't remember all the things she said to me.'

Natalya delivered all this in a kind of level, almost soundless voice.

'And you, Natalya Alexeyevna, what did you say to her?' Rudin asked.

'What did I say to her?' Natalya repeated. 'What are *you* intending to do?'

'My God! My God!' Rudin replied. 'It's so cruel! It's happened so quickly! It's such a sudden blow! ... And your mother really did get in such a state?'

'Yes ... yes, she doesn't want to hear a single thing about you.'

'This is ghastly! So there's no hope at all?'

'None at all.'

'Why should we be made so miserable! That vile bastard, Pandalevsky! ... You were asking me, Natalya Alexeyevna, what I intend to do. My head's in such a whirl, I can't think of a thing ... I can only feel my misery ... I'm astonished at your composure!'

'Do you think I find it easy?' Natalya asked.

Rudin began walking up and down the dam. Natalya did not take her eyes off him.

'Didn't your mother question you about it?' he asked eventually.

'She asked me if I loved you.'

'And you said?'

Natalya said nothing for a moment.

'I did not lie.'

Rudin took her by the hand.

'Always and in everything noble and generous! Oh, the heart of a girl is pure gold! But did your mother declare herself so firmly about the impossibility of our marriage?'

'Yes, quite firmly. I've already told you she's convinced that you're not thinking of marrying me.'

'So she just considers me a cheat! What have I done to deserve that?'

And Rudin clutched at his head.

'Dmitry Nikolaich,' said Natalya, 'we're just wasting our time! Remember, I'm seeing you for the last time. I came here not to cry, not to complain – you can see I'm not crying – I came for advice.'

'But what advice can I give you, Natalya Alexeyevna?'

'What advice? You're a man. I'm used to believing in you,

and I'll believe in you right up to the end. Tell me what you intend to do.'

'My intentions? Your mother'll probably turn me out of the house.'

'Probably. She told me yesterday she'll have to stop knowing you . . . But you're not answering my question.'

'What question?'

'What do you think we ought to do now?'

'What ought we to do?' Rudin replied. 'Submit, of course.'

'Submit,' Natalya repeated slowly and her lips went pale.

'Submit to fate,' Rudin went on. 'There's nothing else for it! I know only too well how bitter, how difficult, how unendurable it can be. But judge for yourself, Natalya Alexeyevna, I'm a poor man . . . true, I could work; but even if I were rich, would you be in a condition to endure the violent rupture with your family and your mother's anger? . . . No, Natalya Alexeyevna, it's not to be contemplated. Evidently you and I are not destined to live together and the happiness of which I dreamed is not for me!'

Natalya suddenly covered her face with her hands and burst into tears. Rudin drew close to her.

'Natalya Alexeyevna! Darling Natalya!' he began passionately. 'Don't cry, for God's sake, don't tear my heart to pieces, please calm yourself . . .'

Natalya raised her head.

'You tell me to calm myself,' she began, and her eyes glistened through her tears. 'I'm not crying about what you think . . . That's not what hurts; what hurts is that I've been deceived in you . . . How could you! I come to you for advice, and at such a moment, and the first thing you say is: submit . . . Submit! So that's the way you put into practice all your talk about freedom, about sacrifices which . . .'

Her voice broke.

'But, Natalya Alexeyevna,' began a confused Rudin, 'remember . . . I'm not denying my words . . . except that . . .'

'You were asking me,' she continued with new force, 'how I answered my mother when she announced she'd rather agree to my death than to my marriage to you: I answered her that I'd rather die than marry anyone else . . . But all you can say is: submit! So she was right: you were just making a joke of me, out of nothing better to do, out of boredom . . .'

'I swear to you, Natalya Alexeyevna . . . I assure you . . .' Rudin insisted.

But she was not listening to him.

'Why on earth didn't you stop me? Why didn't you yourself . . . Or perhaps you weren't reckoning on anything getting in the way? I'm ashamed to talk about it . . . but it's all over anyhow.'

'You must calm yourself, Natalya Alexeyevna,' Rudin started to say, 'we've both got to think out what steps . . .'

'You talked so often about self-sacrifice,' she interrupted, 'but you know if you'd said to me today at once: "I love you, but I can't marry you, I'm not answering for the future, just give me your hand and come away with me," don't you know that I'd have gone with you, I'd have risked everything, don't you? But the truth is that words and deeds are far apart, and you've lost your nerve now exactly as you lost your nerve the day before yesterday at dinner in front of Volyntsev!'

Rudin went red in the face. Natalya's unexpected fervour had astonished him; but her final words hurt his pride.

'You're too overwrought now, Natalya Alexeyevna,' he began, 'you can't appreciate how cruelly you're insulting me. I hope in time you will do me justice; you will understand what it has cost me to renounce a happiness which, as you say yourself, has laid no obligations upon me whatever. Your peace of mind is dearer to me than anything in the world, and I would be the lowest of the low if I were to take advantage of . . .'

'Perhaps, perhaps,' Natalya interrupted, 'perhaps you're

right, and I don't know what I'm saying. But until this moment I've placed such faith in you, I've believed your every word . . . In future, please, do weigh your words, don't scatter them to the wind. When I told you that I loved you I knew the meaning of each word: I really was prepared for anything . . . It now only remains for me to thank you for the lesson and to say good-bye.'

'Stop, for God's sake, Natalya Alexeyevna, I beg you. I don't deserve to be despised by you, I swear to you. Try and see it my way. I'm responsible for you and for myself. If I hadn't loved you most devotedly – why, my God, I'd have proposed at once that you run away with me! . . . Sooner or later your mother'd have forgiven us . . . and then . . . But before thinking of my personal happiness . . .'

He stopped. Natalya's gaze, directed straight at him, confused him.

'You're trying to prove to me that you're an honourable man, Dmitry Nikolaich,' she said, 'and I don't doubt it. You've no capacity for acting from motives of personal gain; but I hardly wanted to be convinced of that, I hardly came here for that reason . . .'

'I hadn't expected, Natalya Alexeyevna . . .'

'Ah! So now it's out! Yes, you hadn't expected all this – you didn't know me. Don't worry . . . you're not in love with me and I'm not throwing myself at anyone.'

'I love you!' exclaimed Rudin.

Natalya drew herself up straight.

'Perhaps. But how do you love me? I remember all your words, Dmitry Nikolaich. Remember how you told me that without complete equality there can be no love . . . You're too lofty for me, you can be no partner of mine . . . It serves me right. You have things to do that are more worthy of you. I won't forget today . . . Good-bye . . .'

'Natalya Alexeyevna, you're not leaving? Surely we won't say good-bye like this?'

He stretched out his hands to her. She stopped. His pleading voice seemed for a moment to make her change her mind.

'No,' she said eventually, 'I feel something inside me has broken . . . I came here and I talked to you just as if I were in a fever; now I must get things straight. This *can't* be, you yourself said it couldn't. My God, as I came here I was mentally saying good-bye to my home and the whole of my past – and for what? Who did I meet here? A faint-hearted man . . . And how did you know I wouldn't be capable of enduring the rupture with my family? "Your mother doesn't agree . . . This is ghastly!" That's all I heard from you. Was it really you, you, Rudin? No! Good-bye . . . Oh, if only you'd really been in love with me, I'd have felt it now, at this moment . . . No, no, good-bye! . . .'

She turned swiftly and ran towards Masha, who had long since begun to get anxious and was making signs at her.

'*You* are the coward, not me!' Rudin shrieked after her.

She no longer paid attention to him and hurried home across the field. She returned safely to her own bedroom; but as soon as she was in the room her strength failed her and she fell senseless into Masha's arms.

But Rudin remained standing a long while on the dam. Finally he shook himself out of his reverie, made his way with slow steps to the path, and walked quietly along it. He was very ashamed of himself . . . and bitter. 'What sort of a girl is she?' he was thinking. 'And at eighteen! . . . No, I didn't know her . . . She's a remarkable girl. What strength of will! . . . She's right: she doesn't deserve the kind of love I felt for her . . . What did I feel?' he asked himself. 'I can hardly feel love any more, can I? So it's ended as it should have done! But how pitiful and insignificant I was in front of her!'

The light clatter of a racing droshky made Rudin raise his eyes. Driving towards him was Lezhnev with his usual trotter. Rudin exchanged a silent bow with him and, as though struck by a sudden thought, turned off the road and walked quickly in the direction of Darya Mikhaylovna's house.

Lezhnev let him go some way, looked after him and, after a moment's thought, also turned his horse round – and travelled back to Volyntsev's where he had spent the night. He found him still asleep, did not order him to be wakened and, in expectation of tea, sat down on the balcony and lit his pipe.

X

VOLYNTSEV rose at about ten o'clock and, having learned that Lezhnev was sitting on his balcony, was very surprised and ordered that he be asked to come to him.

'What happened?' he asked him. 'You'd wanted to go home.'

'Yes, I wanted to, and then I came across Rudin ... All alone, striding through a field, and his face a picture of misery. I turned round and came back.'

'You came back just because you came across Rudin?'

'That is, to tell the truth, I don't really know why I came back; perhaps because I thought about you: I felt I wanted to sit here with you a bit, and there'll still be time for me to get home.'

Volyntsev gave a bitter smile.

'Yes, one can't think of Rudin now without thinking of me ... Be a good fellow!' he shouted loudly, 'bring us some tea!'

The friends began to drink tea. Lezhnev made an effort to talk about farming and a new type of wadded roofing for barns.

Suddenly Volyntsev jumped up from his armchair and struck the table such a blow that the cups and saucers tinkled loudly.

'No!' he cried out. 'I just can't stand this any longer! I'll challenge this clever Dick to a duel, and shoot me he may, or I'll try and plant a bullet in his learned brains!'

'For heaven's sake, don't, don't!' muttered Lezhnev. 'Such a deal of shouting! I even dropped my pipe ... What's wrong with you?'

'What's wrong with me is that I can't be indifferent to the sound of his name. All my blood literally rises up in me.'

'Enough of that, my dear chap, enough of it! You ought to be ashamed!' retorted Lezhnev, picking his pipe up off the floor. 'Forget it! Enough of him!'

'He's insulted me,' Volyntsev went on, walking about the room. 'Yes, he's insulted me! You yourself must agree with that. To start with I didn't come to my senses: he'd caught me unawares; and, after all, who'd have expected a thing like that? But I'll show him he can't play jokes on me ... I'll shoot him, damned philosopher that he is, just as I'd shoot a partridge.'

'A lot of good that'll do you! I'm not even saying this for your sister's sake. Obviously you're madly in love ... so you'd hardly think of your sister! And in regard to the other person, the lady in the case, do you really think that by killing the philosopher you'd put everything right?'

Volyntsev flung himself into an armchair.

'Then I'll go off somewhere! If I stay here grief'll simply break my heart; I simply won't know where to put myself.'

'You'll go away ... now that's another matter! That I will agree with. And do you know what I propose? Let's go together – to the Caucasus or simply to the Ukraine and eat lots of dumplings. My dear chap, that would be splendid!'

'Yes, it would; but who do I leave my sister with?'

'Why doesn't Alexandra Pavlovna come along with us? My God, it'd work out perfectly. The looking after her – that'd be my job! She won't feel the lack of a single thing; if she likes, I'll arrange for someone to serenade her every evening under her window; I'll douse the drivers in eau de cologne and stick flowers along her route. And as for you and me, my dear chap, we'll simply be completely rejuvenated. We'll enjoy ourselves so much, and come home with such enormous bellies, that no love whatever will have a chance of getting us again!'

'You're just joking, Misha!'

'Not at all. That was a brilliant idea of yours.'

'No! Rubbish!' Volyntsev cried again. 'I want to fight him, fight him!'

'That again! What a bad mood you're in today, my dear chap!'

A servant entered with a letter in his hand.

'From whom?' asked Lezhnev.

'From Rudin, Dmitry Nikolayevich. A man came with it from the Lasunskies.'

'From Rudin?' repeated Volyntsev. 'Who is it for?'

'For you, sir.'

'For me . . . let me have it.'

Volyntsev took the letter, quickly broke it open and started reading. Lezhnev watched him attentively and saw an unusual, almost delighted, look of astonishment gather on Volyntsev's face; he dropped his hands.

'What is it?' asked Lezhnev.

'Read it,' said Volyntsev under his breath and passed him the letter.

Lezhnev began reading. This is what Rudin had written:

My dear Sergey Pavlovich,

Today I am leaving Darya Mikhaylovna's house, and I am leaving forever. This will probably surprise you, especially after what happened yesterday. I can't explain to you what it is precisely that makes me take this course; but it somehow seems to me that I should inform you of my departure. You dislike me and even consider me malevolent. I do not intend to justify myself: time will do that. To my way of thinking, it is both unworthy of a man and useless to try showing someone who is prejudiced the injustice of his prejudices. Whoever seeks to understand me will forgive me, but he who does not want to understand me or cannot – that man's accusations do not affect me. I was mistaken about you. In my eyes you remain as before a noble and honourable man; but I supposed you could rise above the surroundings in which you grew up . . . I was wrong. It can't be helped! It's not the first time and it won't be the last. I repeat: I am leaving. I wish you happiness. You will agree that this wish is entirely unselfish, and I hope that you will now be happy. Perhaps in time you will change your opinion of me. Whether we will ever see each other again I do not know, but in any case I remain sincerely and respectfully yours

D.R.

P.S. I will send you the two hundred roubles I owe you as soon as I get back to my estate in Tambov province. I also ask you not to mention this letter to Darya Mikhaylovna.

P.P.S. One final, but important request: since I am now leaving, I hope you will not mention my visit to you in the presence of Natalya Alexeyevna . . .

'Well, what do you make of that?' asked Volyntsev, as soon as Lezhnev had finished the letter.

'What indeed!' exclaimed Lezhnev. 'Shout out loud in Asian fashion: "Allah! Allah!" and then stick a finger in one's mouth in sheer amazement – that's all one can do. He's leaving . . . Well, may his way be smooth! But what's interesting is that he even considered the writing of this letter *as a duty*, and he visited you out of a sense of duty . . . For people like that every step they take's a duty, it's all duty – and debts,' added Lezhnev, pointing with a grin at the P.S.

'But what expressions he comes out with!' exclaimed Volyntsev. 'He was mistaken about me, he expected I'd rise above some surroundings or other . . . What a lot of damned drivel, good Lord! It's worse than verse.'

Lezhnev did not answer; only his eyes smiled.

Volyntsev stood up.

'I want to go to Darya Mikhaylovna's,' he said. 'I want to know what it all means.'

'Wait a moment, my dear fellow, at least give him time to leave. What point is there in your knocking into him again? After all, he's doing a vanishing trick – what more do you want? Better go and lie down and have a sleep. Most likely you spent the whole night tossing and turning from one side to the other. But now everything'll be all right . . .'

'How do you make that out?'

'That's just how it seems to me. Be a good chap, go to

sleep, while I go and see your sister and sit with her for a while.'

'I haven't any wish to go to sleep. Why should I go to sleep? I'd much better ride out and have a look at the fields,' said Volyntsev, tugging at his coat-tails.

'And what a good idea! You go off, my dear fellow, be off with you and have a look at the fields . . .'

And Lezhnev set off for Alexandra Pavlovna's part of the house. He found her in the drawing-room. She greeted him affectionately. She was always delighted to see him; but her face remained sad. She was still bothered by Rudin's visit of the day before.

'Are you from my brother?' she asked Lezhnev. 'How is he today?'

'All right. He's just ridden off to have a look at the fields.'

Alexandra Pavlovna said nothing for a moment.

'Tell me, please,' she began, closely studying the edge of her handkerchief, 'do you know why . . .'

'Rudin came?' Lezhnev finished the question for her. 'I do: he came to say good-bye.'

Alexandra Pavlovna looked up.

'What? To say good-bye?'

'Yes. Haven't you heard? He's leaving Darya Mikhaylovna's.'

'He's leaving?'

'Forever; at least that's what he says.'

'But, I mean, what can one make of that after everything that's . . .'

'That's quite another matter! One can't make head or tail of that, but it is so. Most probably something's happened between them. The string's been stretched too far – and it's snapped.'

'Mikhaylo Mikhaylych!' said Alexandra Pavlovna, 'I don't understand a single thing! It seems to me you're making fun of me . . .'

'As God is my witness I'm not . . . I'm telling you, he's going away and he's informing his acquaintances about it by letter. From a certain point of view, if you like, that's not a bad thing to do. But his departure has upset a certain most remarkable undertaking which your brother and I were just discussing.'

'What was that? What undertaking?'

'It was this. I was proposing to your brother that he go off travelling for pleasure and take you with him. I was going to make it my job to look after you personally . . .'

'That's an excellent idea!' exclaimed Alexandra Pavlovna. 'I can just imagine how you'd look after me. You'd most likely let me die of hunger.'

'You talk like that, Alexandra Pavlovna, because you don't know me. You think I'm a blockhead, a complete blockhead, just wood from the neck up. But don't you know that I'm capable of melting like sugar and spending whole days on my knees?'

'That I confess I'd like to see!'

Lezhnev suddenly stood up.

'Then marry me, Alexandra Pavlovna, and you will see it.'

Alexandra Pavlovna reddened right up to her ears.

'What was that you said, Mikhaylo Mikhaylych?' she repeated in confusion.

'I said something,' answered Lezhnev, 'that has been a long, long while and a thousand times on the tip of my tongue. I've finally said it, and you may do now as you know best. But so as not to embarrass you I'll now leave. If you want to be my wife . . . I'll be out in the garden. If you have no objection, just ask for me to be called: I'll understand . . .'

Alexandra Pavlovna wanted to detain Lezhnev, but he swiftly went out into the garden without putting on his hat, leaned on a gate, and began gazing into the distance.

'Mikhaylo Mikhaylych!' resounded the voice of a maid

137

behind him. 'Please come to the mistress. She's asking for you.'

Mikhaylo Mikhaylych turned round, seized the maid by her head with both hands, to her great astonishment, kissed her on the forehead, and strode off in the direction of Alexandra Pavlovna.

XI

HAVING returned home, immediately after the meeting with Lezhnev, Rudin locked himself in his room and wrote two letters: one to Volyntsev (it is already familiar to the readers) and the other to Natalya. He sat for a long time over this second letter, crossed out and rewrote much of it and, having carefully copied it on to a thin sheet of writing paper, folded it as small as he could and put it in his pocket. With a grief-stricken face he paced up and down his room several times, sat down in an armchair in front of the window and leaned his head on his hand; a tear gently pressed against his eyelashes ... He rose, buttoned up his coat, called for his manservant and ordered him to ask Darya Mikhaylovna whether he might see her.

The man quickly returned and announced that Darya Mikhaylovna requested him to see her. Rudin went to her.

She received him in her study, as on the first occasion, two months ago. But now she was not alone: with her sat Pandalevsky, modest, fresh, spruce, and ingratiating as always.

Darya Mikhaylovna greeted Rudin politely, and Rudin politely bowed to her, but, from no more than a glance at their smiling faces, anyone with the least experience would have understood, even if a word had not been said, that something had gone wrong between them. Rudin knew that Darya Mikhaylovna was angry with him. Darya Mikhaylovna suspected that he already knew everything.

Pandalevsky's news had been very distressing to her. Her high-society haughtiness was aroused. Rudin, an impecunious, unofficial, and so far unknown man, had dared to make assignations with her own daughter – the daughter of Darya Mikhaylovna Lasunsky!

'Granted that he's clever and a genius!' she said. 'But what's that prove? After this anyone in trousers can have hopes of being my son-in-law – does it prove that?'

'It was an age before I could believe my own eyes,' chimed in Pandalevsky. 'How someone could fail to know his own place astonishes me!'

Darya Mikhaylovna became very worked up, and Natalya got the rough edge of her tongue.

She requested Rudin to sit down. He sat down, but no longer like the former Rudin who was almost the master of the house, not even like a good friend, but like a guest, and not a familiar guest at that. All this happened in an instant. Just as instantly can water suddenly be turned into solid ice.

'I have come to you, Darya Mikhaylovna,' Rudin began, 'to thank you for your hospitality. I received news today from my little village and I must go there today without fail.'

Darya Mikhaylovna gazed intently at Rudin.

'He has anticipated me, so he's guessed,' she thought. 'He is relieving me of a tiresome explanation, and so much the better. Long live clever people!'

'Is that so?' she declared loudly. 'Ah, how unpleasant that is! Well, it can't be helped! I hope to see you this coming winter in Moscow. We ourselves will soon be leaving here.'

'I do not know, Darya Mikhaylovna, whether I will be able to get to Moscow; but if I have the funds for it, I will consider it my duty to pay my compliments to you.'

'Aha,' thought Pandalevsky in his turn, 'for a long time, my good man, you've been having everything your own way here as if you owned the place, and now look how you're talking!'

'You, er, perhaps, have received unsatisfactory, er, news from your estate?' he asked with his usual pauses.

'Yes,' answered Rudin drily.

'A poor harvest, perhaps?'

'No, something else . . . Believe me, Darya Mikhaylovna,'

140

Rudin added, 'I will never forget the time I have spent in your house.'

'And I, Dmitry Nikolaich, will always remember with pleasure our acquaintanceship . . . When are you leaving?'

'Today, after dinner.'

'So soon! . . . Well, I wish you a pleasant journey. However, if your affairs don't perhaps detain you too long, you'll still be able to find us here.'

'I hardly think I'll be able to,' Rudin responded and rose to his feet. 'Forgive me,' he added, 'but I am unable at this moment to repay you what I owe you; but as soon as I get to my estate . . .'

'Not a word of that, Dmitry Nikolaich!' Darya Mikhaylovna interrupted him. 'You ought to be ashamed! . . . What time is it?' she asked.

Pandalevsky drew out of the pocket of his jacket a gold watch decorated with enamel and looked at it, carefully squeezing his rosy cheek over a stiff white collar.

'Twenty-seven minutes to three,' he said.

'Time to get changed,' remarked Darya Mikhaylovna. 'Good-bye, Dmitry Nikolaich!'

Rudin rose. The entire conversation between him and Darya Mikhaylovna had borne a special imprint. It had been conducted in the way actors rehearse their parts or diplomats at conferences exchange predetermined phrases . . .

Rudin went out of the room. He knew now from experience how society people do not even cast away but simply drop a man who is no longer any use to them, like a glove dropped after a ball, like a candy wrapping, like a losing ticket in a lottery.

He quickly packed his things and began to wait impatiently for the moment of departure. The entire household was very surprised when they learned of his intentions; even the servants looked at him in bewilderment. Basistov did not disguise his anguish. Natalya openly avoided Rudin. She tried not to look him in the face; he succeeded, however, in pressing his letter into her hand. At dinner Darya Mikhaylovna once again repeated that she hoped to see him before their departure for Moscow, but Rudin said nothing in reply. Pandalevsky made more attempts than anyone to begin a conversation with him. Rudin was frequently assailed by a desire to dash at him and hit him in his florid, ruddy face. Mlle Boncourt kept on peeping at Rudin with a strange, cunning look in her eyes (old, very clever setters sometimes have the same look) as if she seemed to be saying to herself: 'He-he, that's your lot!'

Finally it struck six and Rudin's tarantass was got ready. He began hurriedly making his good-byes. Inwardly he felt awful. He hadn't expected that he would leave this house in this way, as if he were being driven out ... 'How did it all happen like this? And why all the rush? Still, it's all the same in the end,' is what he thought as he bowed on all sides with a forced smile. He glanced for the last time at Natalya and his heart gave a jump: her eyes were directed at him in sad, fare-well reproach.

He ran briskly down the steps and bounded into the taran-tass. Basistov volunteered to accompany him to the first post-station and sat down beside him.

'Do you remember,' began Rudin, as soon as the tarantass had driven out of the courtyard on to a highway lined with fir trees, 'do you remember what Don Quixote said to Sancho Panza after leaving the Duchess's court? "Freedom," he said, "my friend Sancho, is one of a man's most precious posses-sions, and happy is he to whom heaven has given a crust of bread, who has no need to be obliged to another man for it!" What Don Quixote felt then, I feel now ... God grant that you also, my dear Basistov, should experience this feeling some time!'

Basistov squeezed Rudin's hand, and the honest young man's heart beat strongly in his grief-stricken breast. All the way to the post-station Rudin talked about the nobility of man and the meaning of true freedom – he talked passionately, ennoblingly, and in a spirit of truth – and when the moment of parting came Basistov could not contain himself and threw himself on his neck and wept. Rudin also shed a few tears himself; but he did not weep about parting from Basistov, his were tears of self-pity.

Natalya went to her room and read Rudin's letter. He wrote to her:

My dear Natalya Alexeyevna,

I have decided to leave. No other course is open to me. I have decided to leave before I am told quite clearly that I should go. All misunderstandings are likely to cease with my departure; and hardly anyone will regret my going. So why wait? . . . That's that, then; but why should I write to you?

I am parting from you probably for ever, and to leave with you a memory of me even worse than the one I deserve would be too bitter a thing. This is why I am writing to you. I have no wish either to justify myself, or to blame anyone beside myself: I wish, so far as is possible, to offer an explanation of myself . . . The events of the last few days have been so unexpected, so sudden . . .

Today's meeting will serve as a memorable lesson to me. Yes, you are right: I did not know you, but I thought I did! In the course of my life I have had dealings with all kinds of people, and I have had close relations with many women and girls; but, meeting you, I encountered for the first time someone who is *completely* honest and straightforward. I was not accusomed to this, and I did not know how to appreciate you. I felt attracted to you from the first day of knowing you – you may have noticed that. I spent hour after hour with you, and yet I didn't know you; I scarcely even started to know you . . . and yet I could imagine that I was in love with you!! For that sin I am now being punished.

There was a time before when I loved a woman and she loved me. My feeling for her was complex, as was her feeling for me; but because she was not a simple person herself, the feeling suited her. The truth didn't dawn on me then: I haven't recognized it even now, when it's been staring me in the face . . . I did recognize it finally, but then it was too late ... You cannot recapture the past ... Our lives could have been joined – and now they will never be united. How could I prove to you that I could love you with a real love – a love from the heart, not one of the imagination – when I do not myself know whether I am capable of such a love?

Nature has given me much – I know this and I won't start pretending otherwise out of false modesty, particularly now, at such a bitter, such a shameful time for me ... Yes, nature has given me much; but I will die without accomplishing anything worthy of my powers, without leaving behind me any beneficial consequences. All my riches will count for nothing, and I will see no fruit of my seed. I lack ... I can't say exactly what it is I lack ... I lack probably whatever it is without which one cannot drive people's hearts, just as one cannot possess a woman's heart; while power only over people's minds is impermanent and useless. It is my strange, almost comic fate that I am ready to surrender myself completely, greedily, utterly – and yet I can't. I will end by sacrificing myself for some nonsense in which I won't even believe ... My God! At thirty-five still to be trying to set about doing something! ...

I have never told this to anyone else – this is my confession.

But that is enough about me. I want to talk about you and give you some advice: I'm no good for anything else ... You are young; but, no matter how long you live, always follow the promptings of your heart, never submit to your own or another's mind. Believe me, the simpler and tighter the course on which life runs the better; it is not a matter of continually seeking new sides to life but of ensuring that the changes occur at the right time. 'Blessed is he who in youth was young ...'[1] But I realize that this advice refers rather to me than to you.

I confess to you, Natalya Alexeyevna, I'm very depressed. I never deceived myself about the kind of feeling I aroused in Darya Mikhaylovna; but I hoped that I had found at least a temporary lodging ... Now I have to start roaming about the world again. What substitute can I find for your conversation, your presence, your attentive and intelligent gaze? ... I am to blame; but you'll agree that fate has deliberately sniggered at us, as it were. A week ago I would scarcely have guessed that I loved you. The day before yesterday, that evening, in the garden, I heard you say for the first time ... but there's no point in reminding you of what you said then – and now I'm leaving today, leaving with a sense of shame, after a cruel interview with you, carrying away with me not a scrap of hope…. And you still don't know how greatly I am to blame in your eyes … There is some kind of stupid frankness in me, a compulsion to chatter about everything … But there's no point in talking about it! I'm going away for good.

(Here Rudin was on the point of telling Natalya about his visit to Volyntsev, but had second thoughts and erased it, and instead added the second P.S. in his letter to Volyntsev.)

I remain alone on this earth in order to devote myself, as you told me this morning with a cruel smile, to other occupations more suited to me. Alas! If only I could really devote myself to these occupations and finally conquer my apathy … But no! I will remain the same unfinished creature I was before … At the first obstacle I will give up completely; what's happened between us has proved this for me. If only I had at least offered my love as a sacrifice to my future task, my vocation; but I was simply frightened of the responsibility laid upon me and so I proved myself unworthy of you. I am not worth your breaking with your own sphere of life for my sake … But all this is perhaps for the best. From this experience I will perhaps emerge purer and stronger.

I wish you every happiness. Good-bye! Think of me sometimes. I hope you may hear of me again.

Rudin.

Natalya let Rudin's letter drop on to her knee and sat motionless for a long time, staring at the floor. This letter proved to her, more clearly than any possible argument, how right she had been when, saying good-bye to Rudin this morning, she had spontaneously cried out that he did not love her! But this did not make her feel any better. She sat without stirring a muscle: it seemed to her that dark waves had closed noiselessly over her and she was sinking to the bottom, growing cold and still. The first experience of disillusionment is hard for anyone; but for a sincere soul which has no wish to deceive itself and is devoid of frivolity and exaggeration it can be almost unbearable. Natalya remembered her childhood and the times when, out for an evening walk, she always tried to go in the direction of the bright edge of the sky, where the sunset still glowed, and not to the dark. But it was the dark of life that now faced her, and her back was turned to the light ...

Tears rose to Natalya's eyes. Not all tears are beneficial. Glad and wholesome are they when, after gathering in the breast, they eventually flow out – first in a flood, then more easily and all the more sweetly; the dumb pining of regret is ended by them. But there are tears that are cold, niggardly flowing tears: they are squeezed drop by drop from the heart by a heavy and immovable burden of sorrow; they are joyless and bring no comfort. The needy shed that kind of tears, and no man can be considered unhappy who has not shed such tears. Natalya knew what they were like that day.

About two hours went by. Natalya composed herself, rose, wiped her eyes, lit a candle, and burnt Rudin's letter in its flame down to the last bit and threw the ashes out of the window. Then she opened a copy of Pushkin at random and read the first lines that came to hand (she would frequently try telling her fortune this way). This is what she found:

> Whoe'er has felt will feel alarmed
> By phantoms of the days long gone ...
> There are no fascinations left for him,
> Already the serpent of remembering,
> The pangs of conscience will be gnawing him ...[2]

She stood still a moment, surveyed herself with a cold smile in her mirror and, having briefly nodded to herself, went downstairs into the drawing-room.

As soon as she saw her, Darya Mikhaylovna led her into her study, made her sit down beside her, fondly patted her on the cheek and meanwhile looked keenly, almost inquisitively, into her eyes. Darya Mikhaylovna felt secretly at a loss: it had occurred to her for the first time that she really did not know her daughter at all. Having learned from Pandalevsky of her meeting with Rudin, she was not so much angered as surprised by the way in which her sensible Natalya could decide to do such a thing. But when she summoned her to her and started scolding her – not at all as might be expected from a cultured European lady, but fairly raucously and inelegantly – Natalya's firm answers, the resoluteness of her gaze and movements upset Darya Mikhaylovna and even frightened her.

The sudden and also not entirely comprehensible departure of Rudin took a great weight from her heart; but she had expected tears and fits of hysterics . . . Natalya's outward composure was once again disconcerting.

'Well, my child,' began Darya Mikhaylovna, 'how are you now?'

Natalya looked at her mother.

'He's gone . . . the object of your feelings, I mean. Do you not know why he went so quickly?'

'Mother dear,' said Natalya in a quiet voice, 'I give you my word that if you don't breathe a word of it yourself you will never hear a word from me.'

'In that case, you admit you wronged me, do you?'

Natalya lowered her head and repeated:

'You will never hear a word from me.'

'Well, there you are, then!' Darya Mikhaylovna declared with a smile. 'I believe you. But the day before yesterday, don't you remember how . . . Well, no, I won't say anything. It's over, done with and buried. Isn't that right? Now I can recognize you again; but for a moment I was completely nonplussed by you. Well, let me have a kiss, my clever one!'

Natalya raised Darya Mikhaylovna's hand to her lips, and Darya Mikhaylovna kissed her on her bowed head.

'Always listen to my advice, never forget you are a Lasunsky and my daughter,' she added, 'and you will be happy. Now leave me.'

Natalya left without a word. Darya Mikhaylovna gazed after her and thought: 'She's like me – and she'll enjoy herself, *mais elle aura moins d'abandon*.' And Darya Mikhaylovna abandoned herself to recollections of the past . . . the distant past . . .

Afterwards she ordered Mlle Boncourt to be summoned and spent a long time with her behind locked doors. When she dismissed her she asked for Pandalevsky. She wanted urgently to know the real reason for Rudin's departure . . . but Pandalevsky was able to satisfy her completely. That sort of thing was in his line.

The next day Volyntsev and his sister came to dinner. Darya Mikhaylovna had always been very courteous to him, and on this occasion she welcomed him particularly warmly. Natalya was unbearably depressed; but Volyntsev was so polite, so shy in talking to her, that in her soul she could not but be grateful to him.

The day passed quietly, and fairly monotonously, but all of them, on leaving, felt that they had slipped back into their former ways; and that means a great deal, a very great deal.

Yes, all of them had slipped into their former ways . . . all, except Natalya. When she was finally alone she only just managed to drag herself to her bed and, exhausted, brokenhearted, she flung herself face downwards on the pillow. To go on living seemed to her something so bitter, and repugnant, and tasteless, and she was so ashamed of herself, her love, her misery, that at that moment she would probably have agreed to die . . . There awaited her in the future many difficult days, sleepless nights, tiring emotional upheavals; but she was young – life was only just beginning for her, and life sooner or later comes into its own. No matter how heavy a blow fate may have struck someone, that very day he can always have a bite to eat, more the next day – forgive the crudity of the notion – and in that way he'll begin to console himself . . .

Natalya endured torments, and she suffered them for the first time . . . But first sufferings, like first love, are not repeated – thank God!

ABOUT two years had passed. It was the beginning of May. Alexandra Pavlovna, no longer Lipin, but Lezhnev, was sitting on the balcony of her house; it was more than a year since she had married Mikhaylo Mikhaylych. She was as pretty as ever, except that she had grown a little plumper recently. Below the balcony, from which steps led into the garden, a nurse was walking to and fro carrying a red-cheeked baby in a little white coat and a little hat with a white pompon. Alexandra Pavlovna kept on glancing at him. The baby was not crying but solemnly sucking a finger and calmly surveying the world. It was already clear that here was a worthy son for Mikhaylo Mikhaylych.

Our old friend Pigasov was sitting beside Alexandra Pavlovna on the balcony. He had grown noticeably greyer since we last saw him, had become round-shouldered and thin, and he made a whistling sound when he spoke: one of his front teeth had fallen out. The whistling lent even more acerbity to his tirades ... His embittered feelings had not diminished with the years, but his witticisms had lost their point, and he tended to repeat himself more often than he used to. Mikhaylo Mikhaylych was not at home; he was expected back for tea. The sun had already gone down. Where it had set, a strip of pale-gold, lemon colour stretched along the horizon; on the opposite side of the sky there were two stripes: one, the lower, sky-blue, the other, above it, a reddish lilac. Small, light clouds were melting in the heights. Everything promised settled weather.

Suddenly Pigasov burst out laughing.

'What are you laughing at, Afrikan Semyonych?' asked Alexandra Pavlovna.

'Just laughing ... Yesterday I overheard a peasant saying to his wife – she was chattering on about something or other – "Stop your squeakin'!" . . . Now I liked that very much: "Stop your squeakin'!" And as a matter of fact, is there anything a woman can talk sense about? As you know, I never refer to present company. Our ancestors were a lot wiser than we are. In their fairytales the beautiful lady always sits by a window, she has a star on her forehead, but she never utters a word. That's how it should be. But nowadays – judge for yourself: a couple of days ago the wife of the local marshal of nobility told me she didn't like my *bias* – she shot the word straight at my forehead as if she were firing a pistol! Bias, indeed! Well, it would've been a great deal better for her and for all of us, wouldn't it, if through some benevolent re-arrangement of nature she had suddenly been deprived of the use of her tongue?'

'You're just the same as ever, Afrikan Semyonych: still attacking us poor women . . . You know, that really is a great misfortune, after its fashion. I pity you.'

'A great misfortune? What a thing to say! In the first place, it's my opinion that there are only three misfortunes in this world: to spend a winter in a cold house, to wear tight shoes in summer, and to have to sleep in a room with a squalling baby which you can't just sprinkle with some kind of vanishing powder; and in the second place, permit me to say, I have now become quite the most placid of men. You could take me as a shining example – that's how moral a man I am!'

'A good man – well I never! No longer ago than yesterday Yelena Antonovna was complaining to me about you.'

'So that's it! And what was she saying to you, may I ask?'

'She told me that in the course of a whole morning you answered all her questions with "Whatzat, ma'am? Whatzat, ma'am?" and always in such a squawking kind of voice.'

Pigasov roared with laughter.

'You must agree, Alexandra Pavlovna, that was a splendid idea, wasn't it . . . eh?'

'An astonishing idea! How can you be so rude to a woman, Afrikan Semyonych?'

'What? Do you think Yelena Antonovna's a woman?'

'What do you think she is?'

'A drum, for pity's sake, an ordinary drum, the kind you beat with sticks!'

'Ah, yes,' broke in Alexandra Pavlovna, wanting to change the conversation, 'I hear you can be congratulated.'

'On what?'

'On the end of your lawsuit. The Glinov meadows remain yours . . .'

'Yes, they're mine,' Pigasov agreed morosely.

'You've spent so many years trying to get them, and now it's just as if you weren't satisfied.'

'I submit to you, Alexandra Pavlovna,' Pigasov said slowly, 'nothing is worse and more hurtful than a happiness that comes too late. It can give no pleasure, yet it deprives you of that most precious of rights – the right to swear and curse at your fate! Yes, dear lady, a bitter and hurtful thing is a happiness that comes too late.'

Alexandra Pavlovna simply shrugged her shoulders.

'Nanny,' she began, 'I think it's time Misha had a nap. Bring him here.'

And Alexandra Pavlovna busied herself with her son, while Pigasov withdrew, grumbling, to the other corner of the balcony.

Suddenly, not far off, on the road running alongside the garden, Mikhaylo Mikhaylych appeared in his racing droshky. Bounding along in front of his horse were two enormous hounds, one yellow, the other grey, which he had recently acquired. They were ceaselessly biting each other, and yet they were inseparable. A little old dog went out of the gates to meet them, opened its mouth as if on the point of barking, but ended by giving a yawn, and came back, wagging its tail amicably.

'Sasha dear,' cried Lezhnev from a distance, 'look who I'm bringing to see you ...'

Alexandra Pavlovna did not recognize at once the person sitting behind her husband.

'Ah! Mr Basistov!' she exclaimed finally.

'Yes, yes,' answered Lezhnev, 'and what excellent news he's brought! One moment and you'll find out.'

And he drove into the courtyard.

A few moments later he and Basistov appeared on the balcony.

'Hurrah!' he shouted and kissed his wife. 'Seryozha's getting married!'

'To whom?' asked Alexandra Pavlovna excitedly.

'To Natalya, of course ... Our friend's just brought the news from Moscow, and there's a letter for you. Do you hear that, Mishuk?' he added, taking his son into his arms. 'Your uncle's getting married! ... What a phlegmatic rascal you are, doing nothing but batting your eyelids at such news!'

'The young master wants to go to sleep,' the nurse said.

'Yes, ma'am,' said Basistov, approaching Alexandra Pavlovna, 'I've come from Moscow today, on the orders of Darya Mikhaylovna – to revise the accounts for the estate. Here's the letter.'

Alexandra Pavlovna hurriedly broke open her brother's letter. It was only a few lines. In the first access of joy he was informing his sister that he had proposed to Natalya, had received her acceptance and Darya Mikhaylovna's, promised to write more by the first post, and sent greetings and kisses to everyone. He had evidently written the letter in a kind of ecstasy.

Tea was served and Basistov was invited to join them. He was literally deluged with questions. Everyone, even Pigasov, was delighted by the news he had brought.

'Tell us, if you will,' said Lezhnev among other things,

'rumours reached us about a certain Mr Korchagin – was that a lot of nonsense?'

(Korchagin was a handsome young man – a social lion, extraordinarily puffed-up and self-important; he used to adopt unusually majestic poses, as if he were not a living person at all, but his own statue erected by public subscription.)

'Well, no, not completely nonsense,' Basistov replied with a smile. 'Darya Mikhaylovna was very keen on him, but Natalya Alexeyevna couldn't so much as bear to hear his name.'

'Yes, I think I know him,' chimed in Pigasov. 'He's a double-dyed idiot, and noisy with it – for pity's sake! Good heavens, if everyone was like him, one would have to be bribed in a big way before agreeing to live at all!'

'Perhaps,' responded Basistov, 'but in society he has by no means a bit part to play.'

'Well, no matter!' cried Alexandra Pavlovna. 'Enough of him! Oh, how glad I am for my brother! ... And how's Natalya – is she glad, is she happy?'

'Yes, ma'am. She's quite calm, as always – you know how she is – but she seems to be content.'

The evening passed in agreeable and lively talk. They took their places for dinner.

'By the way,' Lezhnev asked Basistov, pouring him some Château-Lafite, 'do you know where Rudin is?'

'I don't know where he is for sure at this moment. He came to Moscow last winter for a short time and then went off to Simbirsk with a family. We wrote to each other for some while: in his last letter he informed me he was leaving Simbirsk – he didn't say where he was going – and since then I haven't heard anything from him.'

'He won't be lost without trace!' said Pigasov. 'He'll be sitting somewhere and preaching. That gentleman'll always find himself two or three disciples who'll listen to him open-mouthed and lend him money. Júst you wait and see, he'll end up by dying somewhere in the back of beyond, in Tsarevokokshaisk or in Chukhloma[1] – in the arms of an exceedingly ancient old maid in a wig who'll be thinking of him as the greatest genius in the world . . .'

'You say very sharp things about him,' Basistov said softly with disapproval.

'Not sharp in the least,' retorted Pigasov, 'but completely justified! In my opinion, he's simply no more than a toady. I forgot to tell you,' he went on, turning to Lezhnev, 'I came across Terlakhov, with whom Rudin went abroad. My, oh my! The things he told me about him, you can't imagine – simply killing! It's remarkable how all Rudin's friends and followers in due course become his enemies.'

'I ask you not to include me among such friends!' Basistov interrupted heatedly.

'Well, you're another matter! I'm not talking about you.'

'What things did Terlakhov tell you?' asked Alexandra Pavlovna.

'A great many things, I can't remember them all. But here's the very best anecdote about Rudin: ceaselessly developing – gentlemen like him are always in a state of development; others simply sleep or eat, for instance, but his sort are in a state of development of taking sleep or food – isn't that so, Mr Basistov?' Basistov did not answer. 'Anyhow, ceaselessly developing, Rudin came to the conclusion with the aid of philosophy that he ought to fall in love. He began to look for a subject worthy of such a startling conclusion. Fortune smiled on him. He got to know a French girl, a very pretty midinette. The whole thing happened in a small German town on the Rhine, I should add. He began to visit her, brought her various books, talked to her about nature and Hegel. Can you imagine the position of the midinette? She thought he was an astronomer. However, you know, though he wasn't much of a chap, still he was a foreigner, a Russian – and she liked him.

Finally he makes an assignation, and a very poetic one: in a gondola on the river. The French girl consented: she dressed up in her best and went for a ride with him in the gondola. They went boating for a couple of hours. And how do you think he occupied all that time? He stroked her hair, gazed thoughtfully at the sky, and repeated a number of times that he had a feeling of paternal tenderness for her. The French girl returned home absolutely frantic and later related the whole thing to Terlakhov. That's the kind of gentleman he is!'

And Pigasov roared with laughter.

'You old cynic!' remarked Alexandra Pavlovna with annoyance. 'But I am more and more convinced that even those who attack Rudin can't say anything really bad about him.'

'Nothing bad? For pity's sake! What about his eternal sponging off others, his borrowings ... Mikhaylo Mikhaylych, he borrowed off you as well, didn't he?'

'Listen, Afrikan Semyonych,' Lezhnev began, and his face acquired a serious look, 'listen: you know, and my wife knows, that lately I've not felt particularly well disposed to Rudin and frequently have even been critical of him. Despite all that' – Lezhnev poured champagne into their glasses – 'this is what I now propose: we've just drunk the health of our dear brother and his fiancée; I now propose that we drink to the health of Dmitry Rudin!'

Alexandra Pavlovna and Pigasov looked at Lezhnev in astonishment, while Basistov, all a-quiver and wide-eyed with wonder, went red with joy.

'I know him well,' Lezhnev went on. 'His defects are well known to me. They are all the more conspicuous because he is not a shallow person.'

'Rudin is a man of genius!' insisted Basistov.

'There is genius in him, admittedly,' rejoined Lezhnev, 'but manliness ... that's the whole problem, there's really no manliness in him. But that's not what matters. I want to talk about what is good and rare in him. He has enthusiasm; and that, believe me – for I speak as a phlegmatic man – is a most precious quality in our time. We have all become intolerably rational, indifferent, and effete; we have gone to sleep, we have grown cold, and we should be grateful to anyone who rouses us and warms us, if only for a moment! It's time to wake up! You remember, Sasha, I was once talking to you about him and I reproached him for his coldness. I was both correct and incorrect in saying that. This coldness is in his blood – through no fault of his – but not in his head. He is not an actor, as I called him previously, not a swindler, not a scoundrel; he lives at someone else's expense not like a sponger, but like a child ... Yes, he will certainly die somewhere in poverty and misery; but is that any reason for us to throw stones at him? He will not achieve anything himself precisely because he has no blood, no manliness; but who has the right to say that he will not contribute, has not already contributed, something useful? That his words have not sown many good seeds in young hearts, to whom nature has not denied, as it has to him, the strength to act, the ability to implement their own ideas? After all, I was the first to experience all this myself ... Sasha knows what Rudin meant to me in my youth. I remember I also asserted that Rudin's words didn't have the capacity to influence people, but I was talking then about people like me, old as I am now, people who've already lived and been broken by life. One false note in a speech – and its entire harmony has vanished for us. But in a young man, fortunately, the hearing is not so highly developed, not so blasé. If the essence of what he hears seems beautiful, what's he care about the tone in which it's said! He'll find the right tone for it within himself.'

'Bravo! Bravo!' exclaimed Basistov. 'How right that is! So far as Rudin's influence is concerned, I swear to you that this man not only had the power to shake you up, he could make you get up and go, he never let you grow settled in your ways, he turned the very foundation of things upside down, he set light to you!'

'Do you hear that?' Lezhnev continued, turning to Pigasov. 'What more proof do you want? You're always attacking philosophy. In talking about it, you can't find sufficiently contemptuous things to say. I don't shed all that many tears for it and I don't understand it all that well; but it isn't from philosophy that our principal troubles stem! Philosophical gobbledygook and hair-splitting will never catch on with Russians: they've got too much common sense for that. But it's impossible to allow, in the name of philosophy, every honourable striving after truth and knowledge to be attacked. Rudin's unhappiness is that he doesn't know Russia, and this is indeed a great unhappiness. Russia can get on without any of us, but not one of us can get on without Russia. Woe to him who thinks so, and double woe to him who really does get along without her! Cosmopolitanism is rubbish, and the cosmopolitan is a nonentity, worse than a nonentity; outside nationality there is no art, no truth, no life, nothing. Without a physiognomy there is not even an ideal face; only a commonplace face is possible in such circumstances. But I will repeat that this is not Rudin's fault: it is his fate, a bitter, hard fate, for which we shall not blame him. We should have to go a long way to find out why such people as Rudin appear in our midst. We shall simply be grateful to him for the good that is in him. That is easier than being unjust to him; and we have been unjust to him. It's not our business to punish him, and there's no need to: he has punished himself far more severely than he ever deserved . . . And God grant that the unhappiness should drive all the bad out of him and leave only the beautiful! I drink Rudin's health! I drink to the health of a comrade of my best years, I drink to youth, its hopes, its strivings, its trustfulness, its honesty, to everything that made our hearts beat fast at twenty and which was better than anything else we've ever known – and are ever likely to know – in our lives . . . I drink to you, golden springtime of our lives, I drink Rudin's health!'

All clinked their glasses with Lezhnev. Basistov in his zeal almost broke his and swallowed the champagne at a gulp, while Alexandra Pavlovna squeezed Lezhnev's hand.

'Mikhaylo Mikhaylych, I'd never suspected you could be so eloquent,' remarked Pigasov. 'You could stand comparison with Mr Rudin himself; even I was touched.'

'I am not at all the eloquent kind,' retorted Lezhnev not without vexation, 'and there's nothing remarkable, I think, in having touched you. Besides, that's enough about Rudin. Let's talk about something else . . . Does . . . what's he called? . . . does Pandalevsky still live at Darya Mikhaylovna's?' he added, turning to Basistov.

'Oh, yes, he's still with her! She's got him a very good job.'

Lezhnev grinned broadly.

'Now there's a chap who won't die in poverty, you can count on that!'

The dinner ended. The guests went their separate ways. Left alone with her husband, Alexandra Pavlovna looked with a smile into his face.

'How well you put things this evening, Misha!' she said, stroking his head. 'What clever and noble things you said! But you must admit you were a little carried away in your praise of Rudin, just as before you were a little carried away against him . . .'

'You don't kick a man when he's down . . . but before I was frightened that he might turn your head.'

'No,' Alexandra Pavlovna responded quite simply, 'he always seemed to me too academic, I was frightened of him and didn't know what to say in his presence. But didn't Pigasov have some fairly wicked things to say about him this evening?'

'Pigasov?' said Lezhnev. 'It was precisely because Pigasov was here that I spoke up so heatedly for Rudin. He dares to call Rudin a toady! In my opinion, his role, Pigasov's role, is a hundred times worse. He's got an independent income, he hasn't got a good word for anyone – but just look how he sucks up to titled people and the rich! Did you know that this Pigasov, who abuses everything and everybody with such bitterness, and makes attacks on philosophy and on women – did you know that when he was in government service he used to take bribes, and sizeable ones! Ah! Now that's food for thought!'

'Are you sure?' exclaimed Alexandra Pavlovna. 'I'd never've expected that! ... Listen, Misha,' she added after a pause, 'I want to ask you ...'

'What?'

'Do you think my brother'll be happy with Natalya?'

'How can I say ... there's every probability ... She'll be in charge – between ourselves we don't have to make a secret of that – because she's cleverer than he is; but he's a splendid chap and loves her with all his heart. What more can one ask? After all, we love one another and we're happy, aren't we?'

Alexandra Pavlovna smiled and squeezed his hand tightly.

That very same day, when everything we have narrated was occurring in Alexandra Pavlovna's house, in one of the remote provinces of Russia, in the midday heat, a wretched little bass-wood cart harnessed with a trio of local peasant horses dragged itself slowly along a wide highway. Sitting up on the driving board, with his legs astride the swingle-tree, was a grey-haired little peasant in a tattered cloth coat who time and again gave the rope reins a shake and waved a whip; while in the cart itself, sitting on a flat-looking trunk, was a tall man in a peak-cap and an old, dust-covered cloak. This was Rudin. He sat with bent head and the peak of his cap drawn over his eyes. The irregular jolting of the cart threw him from side to side and he seemed completely dead to the world, as if he were dozing. Eventually he straightened himself.

'When on earth are we going to get to the post-station?' he asked the peasant sitting up on the driving board.

''s like this, sir, it is,' said the peasant and gave a stronger tug at the reins, 'when we get up that 'ill there'll be no more'n a mile to go . . . Hey, you there! Mind now . . . I'll mind you, I will,' he added in a thin voice, giving the right-hand horse a taste of the whip.

'You seem to be making very poor time,' Rudin remarked. 'We've been crawling along since morning and simply don't seem to be able to get there. You might at least sing something.'

'There's nothin's to be done about it, sir! See for yoursen, the 'orses are all worn out . . . It's the heat again. An' I'm not a singin' man, I'm not one o' them cabbies . . . Mutton-head, hey mutton-head!' the little peasant suddenly shouted, addressing a passer-by in a short brown coat and dilapidated bast footwear. 'Get out of the way, mutton-head!'

'Look out yourself . . . so-called driver!' muttered the passer-by in his wake and came to a stop. 'Moscow hayseed!' he added in a voice brimming with reproach, shook his head, and went hobbling on his way.

'An' where might you be off to?' struck up the little peasant in his drawling way, giving the shaft-horse a tug. 'Ah, you're a sly one! A real sly one, for sure!'

The exhausted horses somehow eventually reached the post-station. Rudin stepped out of the cart, paid off the peasant (who didn't bow to him and shook the money about for a long time in his palm as a sign that he found the tip too small), and carried his trunk into the post-station by himself.

One of my acquaintances who has spent much of his life travelling about Russia has made the observation that if the walls of a post-station waiting-room are hung with pictures depicting scenes from *The Prisoner of the Caucasus*[2] or portraits of Russian generals, then horses may be obtained easily; but if there are pictures of the life of the well-known gambler Georges de Germany,[3] then the traveller can abandon hope of a quick departure: he will have time to admire the upstanding quiff of hair, the white waistcoat, and unusually narrow and short breeches of the gambler in his youth and his frenzied face when, already an old man, waving aloft a chair in a cottage room with a steeply pitched ceiling, he beats his son to death. These pictures from 'Thirty Years, or The Life of a Gambler' were precisely those hanging in the room which Rudin entered. In answer to his shout the station-master appeared, half-asleep (by the way, has anyone ever seen a station-master who wasn't half-asleep?) and, without even waiting for Rudin's question, announced in a tired drawl that there were no horses to be had.

'How can you say there aren't any horses,' said Rudin 'when you don't even know where I'm going? I came here by local peasant ones.'

'We haven't got any horses for going anywhere,' answered the station-master. 'And where are you going?'

'To —sk.'

'There aren't any horses,' repeated the station-master and went out of the room.

In annoyance Rudin went over to the window and flung his cap down on the table. He had not changed greatly, but he had grown sallower in the past two years; threads of silver shone here and there in his curly hair, and his eyes, though still beautiful, seemed less brilliant; fine wrinkles, the traces of bitter and anguished feelings, had gathered about his lips, on his cheeks, on his temples.

His clothes were worn and old, and he gave no appearance of having any white linen. The time of his full bloom had evidently passed; as gardeners say, he had gone to seed.

He started reading the titles to the pictures on the walls – a well-known pastime of all bored travellers. Suddenly the door creaked and the station-master came in.

'There are no horses for —sk, and there won't be for a long time,' he began, 'but there are some returning to —ov'.

'Returning to —ov,' cried Rudin. 'For heaven's sake that's not my way at all! I'm going to Penza, but —ov, I think, is in the direction of Tambov.'

'What about it? You can go on there from Tambov or you can turn off at —ov.'

Rudin gave it some thought.

'Oh, well, so be it,' he said finally, 'order the horses to be harnessed. It doesn't matter. I'll go to Tambov.'

The horses were quickly got ready. Rudin carried out his trunk, climbed into the cart, sat down, and let his head loll forward in a doze as before. There was something helpless and forlornly submissive in his hunched figure . . . And the troika of horses went off at a slow trot, the little harness bells shrilly ringing.

Epilogue

SEVERAL more years passed.

It was a cold autumn day. A carriage drove up to the porch of the chief hotel of the provincial town of S—; there climbed out of it, slightly straining and grunting, a gentleman who was not yet elderly but who had already succeeded in acquiring that stoutness of build which people are accustomed to call a mark of respectability. Having climbed the stairs to the first floor, he stopped at the entrance to a wide corridor and, seeing no one there to look after him, asked in a loud voice for a room. A door banged somewhere and from behind low screens jumped a tall flunkey who dashed on ahead of him with a brisk, crabwise motion, the shiny back of his coat and his rolled-up sleeves glistening in the murk of the corridor. As soon as he reached his room the new arrival flung off his greatcoat and scarf, sat down on the sofa and, resting his clenched hands on his knees, first of all looked around him, as if not fully awake, and then called for his manservant. The flunkey made a compliant movement and vanished. The new arrival was none other than Lezhnev. Work in connection with army recruitment had brought him into S— from the country.

Lezhnev's manservant, a young chap, curly-haired and red-cheeked, dressed in a grey greatcoat, tied round the waist with a sky-blue sash, and wearing soft felt boots, entered the room.

'Well, my good fellow, we've finally got here,' said Lezhnev, 'and you were frightened all the time that the wheel would lose its metal tyre.'

'Yes, we've got here!' agreed the manservant, endeavouring to smile above the raised collar of the greatcoat. 'But the tyre didn't jump off because . . .'

'Anyone in here?' a voice resounded in the corridor.

Lezhnev shuddered and pricked up his ears.

'Hey! Who's there?' the voice repeated.

Lezhnev stood up, went to the door, and swiftly opened it.

In front of him stood a tall man, almost completely grey and bent with age, in an ancient velveteen jacket with bronze buttons. Lezhnev recognized him at once.

'Rudin!' he exclaimed with great emotion.

Rudin turned round. He was unable to make out Lezhnev's features, standing as he was with his back to the light, and looked at him in bewilderment.

'Don't you recognize me?' Lezhnev began by asking.

'Mikhaylo Mikaylych!' exclaimed Rudin and held out a hand, but became confused and was on the point of withdrawing it.

Lezhnev quickly seized it with both hands.

'Come in, come in!' he said to Rudin and led him into his room.

'How you've changed!' Lezhnev declared after a moment's silence and in a subdued voice.

'Yes, that's what they say!' responded Rudin, letting his gaze wander round the room. 'The years take their toll ... While you've not changed at all. How is Alexandra ... how is your wife?'

'Thank you very much for asking, she's very well. But what stroke of fortune brings you here?'

'What brings me here? That's a long story. Actually I'm here quite by chance. I was looking for an old friend. However, I'm very glad ...'

'Where are you having dinner?'

'Where am I having dinner? I don't know. At an inn somewhere. I've got to leave town today.'

'Got to?'

Rudin gave a meaningful smile.

'Yes, my dear sir, got to. I am being exiled to my estate.'

'Have dinner with me.'

For the first time Rudin looked Lezhnev directly in the eyes.

'You are really asking me to have dinner with you?' he asked.

'Yes, Rudin, in a comradely spirit, in memory of old times. Would you like that? I didn't expect to meet you, and God knows when we'll meet again. We can't just say good-bye like this!'

'Put like that, I agree.'

Lezhnev pressed Rudin's hand, summoned his manservant, ordered dinner and commanded that a bottle of champagne be put on ice.

In the course of the dinner Lezhnev and Rudin, like a couple of conspirators, talked all the time about their student days and recalled many things and many people, alive and dead. To start with Rudin spoke unwillingly, but he drank a few glasses of wine and the blood soon ran hotly in his veins. Eventually the flunkey removed the last dish. Lezhnev rose, locked the door and, returning to the table, sat down directly opposite Rudin and calmly rested his chin on his two hands.

'Well, the time's come,' he began, 'for you to tell me everything that's happened to you since I last saw you.'

Rudin looked at Lezhnev.

'My God,' Lezhnev thought again, 'how he's changed, poor fellow!'

Rudin's features had changed little, especially since the time we saw him at the post-station, although the stamp of approaching age had already left its mark upon them; but their expression was quite different. The eyes had another kind of look; his whole being, his movements – slow at one moment, disconnectedly jerky the next – his broken speech, devoid of all warmth, expressed an ultimate exhaustion of spirit, a secret and unspoken misery far removed from that half-pretended

166

melancholy which he used to parade on occasion and which is generally the prerogative of young men full of hope and self-confident ambition.

'Tell you everything that's happened to me, eh?' he began. 'It's impossible to tell everything and it isn't worth it . . . I've done many things, wandering about not only physically but in spirit as well. The things and the people I've been disenchanted by, my God! The people I've got to know! The people!' Rudin repeated, noting that Lezhnev was watching him with particular sympathy. 'How many times my own words became repugnant to me – I'm not talking about the sound of them on my own lips but on the lips of people who shared my opinions! How many times I've run the gamut from the irritability of a child to the mindless insensitivity of a horse which doesn't even flick its tail when you flog it . . . How many times I've been overjoyed, full of hope, full of enmity and full of despair – all for nothing! How many times I've begun by soaring like a falcon – and ended at a crawl, like a snail with its shell crushed! . . . The places I've been, the paths I've trod! And paths can be muddy,' added Rudin and slightly turned away. 'You know . . .' he went on . . .

'Listen a moment,' Lezhnev interrupted him, 'at one time we used to call each other Mitya and Misha . . . Shall we? Let's revive the past, let's drink to Mitya and Misha!'

Rudin was deeply touched and rose for the toast, and there flashed in his eyes an emotion which cannot be put into words.

'Let's drink,' he said. 'Thank you, my dear fellow, let's drink.'

Lezhnev and Rudin drained their glasses.

'You know, Misha,' Rudin began saying, smiling and specially emphasizing the *Misha*, 'I have a worm in me that goes on gnawing at me and devouring me and will never let me rest. It shoves me up against people – they begin by submitting to my influence, but afterwards . . .'

Rudin passed his hand through the air.

'Since I last saw you, Mikhaylo ... er, Misha, I've re-experienced and rediscovered a great deal ... I've started living again, started on something new twenty times over – and just look where it's got me!'

'Mitya, my dear fellow, you just didn't have the staying power,' said Lezhnev, as if to himself.

'You're right, Misha, I didn't have the staying power! I didn't know how to build anything; and a lot of good there is in trying to build something, my dear chap, when you've got no firm ground under you, when you ought really to start by creating your own personal foundations! I won't try to describe all my travels – all my failures, that is, speaking truthfully. I'll tell you two or three episodes ... those episodes in my life when it seemed that success had just smiled on me, or no, when I began to hope for success – which is not quite the same thing ...'

Rudin swept back his sparse grey hair with the same movement of the hand that he had used when his locks had been dark and abundant.

'Well, here goes,' he began. 'In Moscow I got to know a rather strange gentleman. He was very rich and owned extensive estates; he was not in government service. His chief and only passion was a love of science, of science in general. I still can't make out why he should've conceived this passion! It suited him about as well as a saddle suits a cow. He himself could only keep abreast of things of the mind with considerable effort and scarcely knew how to talk, but simply used to move his eyes about expressively and nod his head knowingly. My dear Misha, I've never yet met a nature less talented or poorer than his ... In Smolensk province there are places like that – sand and nothing else, just the occasional tuft of grass that no animal would think of eating. Nothing came easily to him, everything just slipped away from him; and yet he still remained crazy about making everything easy difficult. If he'd been in charge of things, he'd have had everyone eating with their heels – and that's the truth! He worked, he wrote, and he read untiringly. He wooed science with a kind of stiff-necked persistence, with awful perseverance; he had enorm-ous ambition and an iron character. He lived alone and he was reputed to be eccentric. I got to know him ... well, he liked me. I confess I saw through him soon enough, but his zeal touched me. Besides, he had such means, with his help so much good could be done, so many actually worthwhile things could be brought in ... I settled in his house and eventually accompanied him to his country estate. I had vast plans, my dear Misha: I dreamed of various splendid improve-ments and innovations ...'

'As at Darya Lasunsky's, remember,' remarked Lezhnev with a good-natured smile.

'Not like that! There I knew, in my soul, that nothing would come of my words; but here ... here a quite different field of activity opened up before me ... I brought with me some books on agronomy – true, I'd not read a single one of them right through to the end – and, well, I set about apply-ing them in practice. At first nothing worked, as I'd expected, but later it looked as if things had got going. My newfound friend wouldn't commit himself and just watched, without interfering – that is, to a certain extent he didn't interfere. He would accept my proposals and implement them, but against his will, grudgingly and with a secret mistrustfulness, and he would bend everything his own way. He was extraordinarily fond of his own ideas. He'd get hold of one of his ideas with great effort, like a ladybird climbing on to a blade of grass, and he'd sit on it and sit on it, all the time spreading his wings and making ready to fly – and then he'd suddenly fall off and have to start climbing up again ... Don't be surprised at all these comparisons. Even then they came bubbling up within me. Anyhow, that's how I struggled on for a couple of years. Despite all my fuss and bother things went badly. I began to grow tired, my friend bored me, I started being caustic, he weighed down on me just like a feather-bed; his mistrustfulness turned into unspoken irritability, feelings of hostility possessed the two of us and we simply couldn't say anything to each other; he strove covertly, but ceaselessly, to show that he wasn't under my influence, and my arrangements were either altered out of all recognition or countermanded completely ... I noticed eventually that I was staying with my gentlemanly landowner in the capacity of a hanger-on who could provide some intellectual exercise. I grew bitter at such a waste of time and effort, and I felt bitter that I'd once again been deceived in my expectations. I knew very well what I was losing in going away; but I couldn't be at peace with myself, and one day, as a consequence of a painful and disgraceful scene which I witnessed and which showed up my friend in a far too unprofitable light, I quarrelled with him once and for all and left him, abandoning this milord fashioned out of local Russian flour with an admixture of German treacle ...'

'That is to say, you abandoned your source of daily bread,' said Lezhnev placing both hands on Rudin's shoulders.

'Yes, and I found myself once again light as air and bare as a babe in empty space. Fly, then, wherever you want ... Oh, let's have a drink!'

'To your health,' said Lezhnev, rose, and kissed Rudin on the forehead. 'To your health and in memory of Pokorsky ... He also knew how to remain a beggar.'

'So that was the first of my travels,' Rudin began after a short pause. 'Do you want me to go on?'

'Please go on.'

'Ah, well! But even talking's a bore. I'm tired of talking, my dear chap ... However, so be it. Having gone the rounds of several places ... Incidentally, I could tell you how I became a secretary to a well-intentioned dignitary and what came of it, but that would take us too far from the point ... Having gone the rounds of several places, I decided to turn myself finally – don't laugh, please – into a businessman, into a practical fellow. It turned out like this: I took up with a certain – you may perhaps have heard of him – a certain Kurbeyev – do you know him?'

'No, I haven't heard of him. But Mitya, for pity's sake, you, with your mind, could've guessed couldn't you that your business wasn't to be – forgive the pun – a businessman?'

'I know, my dear Misha, that it's not my business; but then what is my business? . . . But if only you'd seen Kurbeyev! Please don't imagine he was some empty loud-mouth. They say I used to be eloquent. By comparison with him I simply didn't mean a thing. This was a man of extraordinary learning, knowledgeable, with a really creative head, my dear chap, for industrial and business matters. His mind seethed with the boldest and most unexpected plans. We joined forces and decided to devote our energies to a matter of general utility . . .'

'What, may I ask?'

Rudin lowered his eyes.

'You will laugh.'

'Why should I? No, I won't laugh.'

'We decided to make a river in — province navigable,' said Rudin with an awkward smile.

'So that's it! This Kurbeyev, then, was a man of capital?'

'He was poorer than me,' retorted Rudin and gently lowered his grey head.

Lezhnev burst out laughing, but suddenly stopped and seized Rudin's hand.

'Please forgive me, Mitya,' he said, 'but I just hadn't expected that. Well, this undertaking of yours stayed on paper in that case, did it?'

'Not quite. A start was made. We hired workers . . . and, well, we got going. But at this point various obstacles were encountered. In the first place, the owners of the water-mills didn't want to know what we were up to, and above all we couldn't deal with the water without machinery and there wasn't any money for machinery. For six months we lived rough in dug-outs. Kurbeyev lived off nothing but bread, and I also lived on basic rations. However, I don't regret it: the scenery in those parts is astonishingly beautiful. We struggled on and on, trying to cajole merchants, writing letters, sending round petitions. It ended by my sinking my last penny in it.'

'Well,' remarked Lezhnev, 'I think it wasn't too hard for you to sink your last penny in it!'

'Exactly, it wasn't too hard.'

Rudin glanced out of the window.

'But it wasn't a bad plan, by God, and could've yielded enormous benefits.'

'Where's this Kurbeyev got to?' asked Lezhnev.

'Where's he got to? He's in Siberia now, he's become the owner of a goldmine. And you'll see, Misha, he'll make his pile, he won't fail.'

'That may be; but you're not likely to make yours.'

'I'm not likely to? So what! However, I know I've always been a futile person in your eyes.'

'You, Mitya? That's enough, my dear chap! . . . There was a time, it's true, when all I could see were your bad sides; but now, believe me, I've learned to appreciate you. You won't make your pile . . . For pity's sake, I love you for that!'

Rudin gave a feeble grin.

'Really?'

'I respect you for it!' repeated Lezhnev. 'Do you understand me?'

They were both silent.

'Well, shall I move on to the third of my travels?' asked Rudin.

'Please do.'

'Very well. The third and last. I've only just parted company with this one. But mightn't I have bored you?'

'Go on, go on.'

'You see, Misha, it was like this,' Rudin began, 'I was once thinking at leisure ... I've always had a lot of leisure ... I was thinking: I know a fair number of things, I've a desire to do good ... Listen, Misha, you won't deny my desire to do good, will you?'

'Of course not!'

'I'd more or less come unstuck in all the other things I'd done ... Why shouldn't I become a pedagogue or, to put it plainly, a teacher ... rather than live as I had, pointlessly ...'

Rudin stopped and sighed.

'Rather than live pointlessly, wouldn't it be better to try and pass on what I knew to others: perhaps they could derive at least a certain benefit from my knowledge. In the last resort my capabilities are exceptional and I know how to use my tongue ... So I decided to devote myself to this new business. I busied myself trying to find a job; I didn't want to give private lessons; and primary schools weren't the place for me. Finally I succeeded in getting a teaching job in the local high school.'

'Teaching what?' asked Lezhnev.

'Teaching Russian literature. I will tell you something – I've never undertaken anything with such enthusiasm as I did this. The thought of being able to influence young people inspired me. I spent three weeks composing my introductory lecture.'

'Have you got it with you?' interrupted Lezhnev.

'No, it got put away somewhere. It didn't come off badly and it pleased them. I can see them now, the faces of my audience – good young faces with expressions of straightforward attention, eager concern, and even astonishment. I climbed on to the rostrum and gave my lecture in a fever of excitement; I thought it would last an hour or more, but I'd finished it in twenty minutes. The school inspector was sitting there – a dry old stick wearing silver-rimmed spectacles and a short wig – and he occasionally inclined his head in my direction. When I finished and jumped down from the rostrum he said to me: "Good, my dear sir, but a bit high-flown and obscure, and not much about the subject." But the pupils followed me respectfully with their eyes ... truthfully. That's what makes youth so precious! I brought my second lecture in written form, and my third ... after that I began to improvise.'

'And you were a success?' asked Lezhnev.

'A great success. My audiences came in droves. I conveyed to them everything in my soul. Among them were three or four really remarkable boys; the others didn't understand me all that well. However, I've got to admit that those who understood me sometimes embarrassed me with their questions. But I wasn't disheartened. They all grew very fond of me; and in the exams I gave them all full marks. But at this point an intrigue was hatched against me ... or no, there wasn't any intrigue, but I simply found myself like a fish out of water! I was getting in other people's way and they were crowding me out. I gave lectures to schoolboys that wouldn't always be given to students; my audiences gained little from them ... I didn't know the facts well enough. Besides, I couldn't be satisfied by the round of activities to which I'd been appointed ... as you know, Misha, that's always been my weakness. I wanted to make radical changes, and I swear to you that these changes would've been both practical and easy. I hoped to bring them about through the help of the headmaster, an honest and good man, over whom I had some influence to start with. His wife was on my side. In my life, my dear Misha, I've not met many women like her. She was approaching forty; but she had faith in human goodness, loved all things beautiful just like a fifteen-year-old girl, and was never frightened of expressing her convictions in front of anyone. I will never forget her high-minded enthusiasm and purity. On her advice I drew up a plan ... But at this point I had the ground taken from under me and I was blackened in her eyes. My reputation was particularly damaged by the mathematics teacher, a petty man, sharp-tongued, bilious, and without beliefs of any kind, rather like Pigasov, only much more business-like than him ... By the way, is Pigasov still alive?'

'He's still alive and, just imagine, married to a real *bourgeoise* who beats him, so rumour has it.'

'Go on! And is Natalya Alexeyevna well?'

'Yes.'

'Is she happy?'

'Yes.'

Rudin was silent a moment.

'What was I talking about ... Oh, yes, about the mathematics teacher! He loathed me, compared my lectures to firework displays, he would seize upon every slightly unclear expression of mine and once caught me out over some monument of the sixteenth century ... But the chief thing was that he cast doubt on my good intentions; my final ambitious soap bubble came up against him, like a needle, and burst. The school inspector, whom I didn't get on with right at the start, incited the headmaster against me; there was a scene, I didn't want to give way, grew heated, and the matter went to higher authority; I was forced into resigning. I didn't limit myself to that, I wanted to show that I couldn't be treated in such a way ... but I could be treated in any way they liked ... So I've now got to leave here.'

A silence ensued. Both friends remained sitting with bowed heads.

Rudin was the first to start speaking.

'Yes, my dear chap,' he began, 'I can now say with Koltsov:

> O where have you brought me to, my youth,
> To the point where I'm doomed to stay put ...[1]

And yet was I really fit for nothing, was there really nothing on this earth I could do? I've often asked myself that question, and no matter how much I've tried to humble myself in my own eyes I couldn't but feel in myself the presence of powers which are not given to all people! Why do these powers remain fruitless? And there's another thing. You remember, Misha, when you and I were abroad, I was bumptious and false in those days ... It was exactly as though in those days I had no clear idea what I wanted and I was carried away with words and believed in phantoms; but now, I swear to you, I can proclaim loudly, before all, what I want. I've got absolutely nothing to hide: I am completely – in the purest sense of the word – loyal; I am reconciled to being that, I want to apply myself to existing circumstances, I don't want much, I just want to attain something in the short term, to be if only of trivial use. But no! Nothing succeeds! What's this mean? What prevents me from living and behaving like others? That's all I can speculate about now. I've hardly succeeded in reaching a definite position or stopping at a known point of view when fate just drags me down from it ... I've begun to be frightened of it – my fate, that is ... Why should it all be like this? Answer me this riddle!'

'Riddle!' repeated Lezhnev. 'Yes, it's true. You were always a riddle to me, my dear Mitya. Even in our young days when, after some trivial prank, you'd suddenly start talking so eloquently that my heart would quiver, and then once again you'd start – well, you know what I mean – even then I didn't understand you, which is why I stopped being friends with you ... You've got so many powers and such an indefatigable striving towards an ideal ...'

'It's words, all words! There were no actions!' Rudin interrupted.

'No actions! Whatever actions ...'

'What actions? Supporting by the sweat of your own brow a blind old woman and her entire family, like our friend Pryazhentsev ... That's what I mean by actions, Misha.'

'Yes; but the right word in the right place is also an action.'

Rudin looked at Lezhnev in silence and gently shook his head. Lezhnev had been on the point of saying something and drew his hand across his face.

'So you're off to your village, then, are you?' he asked finally.

'To my village.'

'Have you still got it?'

'Something's left of it. Two and a half serfs. A corner in which to die. You're probably thinking, Misha: "Even now he can't get by without phrase-mongering!" True, phrase-mongering's been my downfall, it's been the death of me and I still can't give it up. But what I said wasn't phrase-mongering. These white hairs, these wrinkles, these holes at the elbows aren't phrase-mongering, my dear Misha. You've always been hard on me and you were right; but it's not a question of being severe now, when everything's already finished and there's no oil left in the lamp and the lamp itself is cracked and the wick'll be burnt out in a moment . . . Death, my friend, must bring peace at the end . . .'

Lezhnev jumped up.

'Mitya!' he cried. 'Why're you talking to me like this? What have I done to deserve this from you? What sort of a judge of things would I be, and what sort of a man would I be if, at the sight of your sunken cheeks and your wrinkles, the word *phrase-mongering* could enter my head? You want to know what I think of you? Very well. I am thinking: Here's a man – with his capabilities what mightn't he have achieved, what earthly riches mightn't he have possessed now, had he wished! – but I find him starving, with nowhere to live . . .'

'I rouse your compassion,' murmured Rudin in a hollow voice.

'No, you're wrong. You rouse my respect – that's what. Who prevented you from spending years and years with this landowner, your friend, who, I'm quite sure, would've ensured you an income if only you'd been content to suck up to him? Why is it you couldn't fit in with things at the high school, why is it that you – strange chap that you are! – no matter with what grand idea you embark on a project, end it every time without exception by sacrificing your own personal interests, by not putting your roots down in unfriendly soil no matter how rich it might be?'

'I was born a rolling stone,' Rudin went on with a despondent smile. 'I can't stop myself.'

'That's true; but you can't stop yourself not because there's a worm in you, as you said at the beginning of our conversation ... It's not a worm that gnaws at you, not a spirit of empty restlessness, it's the fire of the love of truth that burns within you, and evidently it burns, despite all your tribulations, more strongly in you than in many who do not even consider themselves egoists and who would no doubt call you an intriguer. I would have been the first in your place to have silenced that worm long ago and to have made peace with the world; but you've not even become more embittered and I'm sure this very day, Mitya, this very moment you're ready to start once again on a new project just like any young man.'

'No, my dear chap, I'm tired now,' said Rudin. 'I've had enough.'

'Tired, indeed! Another man would have died long ago. You say that death brings peace, while life, you suppose, doesn't? The man who has lived and not become tolerant of others doesn't deserve tolerance in return. Is there a man alive who can say he doesn't need tolerance? You've done what you can, struggled as best you could ... What more can one ask for? We have gone our separate ways ...'

'You, Misha, are an entirely different person from me,' Rudin interrupted with a sigh.

'We've gone our different ways,' Lezhnev continued, 'perhaps precisely because, thanks to my income, my cold-blooded nature, and other happy circumstances, nothing has prevented me from sitting in one spot and remaining a spectator of life, with my arms folded, while you had to go out into the fields, roll up your sleeves, and earn your keep by working. We've gone different ways ... but just look how close we are to each other. You and I speak the same language, half a hint's enough for us to understand each other, we were brought up on the same feelings. And there aren't very many of us left, my dear chap; we're the last of the Mohicans! We could go our different ways, even have our enmities in those far-off years when so much of life still remained ahead of us; but now, when the crowd around us is thinning, when new generations are marching past us towards our very goals, we must hold tighter to one another. Let's drink a toast to that, Mitya, and sing as we used to: *Gaudeamus igitur!*'

The friends clinked glasses and sang the old-fashioned student song in deeply emotional and flat, absolutely Russian voices.

'You're now off to your village,' Lezhnev began again. 'I don't think you'll stay there long, and I can't imagine how, where, and as what you'll end up ... But remember: no matter what happens to you, you always have a place, a nest, where you can hide. It's my house ... do you hear that, old fellow? Philosophy also has its invalids: they need to have a home to go to.'

Rudin stood up.

'Thank you, my dear chap,' he went on. 'Thank you! I won't forget you for this. A home is just what I don't deserve. I've spoilt my life and not served philosophy as I should ...'

'Be quiet!' continued Lezhnev. 'Everyone remains as nature made him, and you can't ask more of him than that! You called yourself the Wandering Jew ... Who's to know, perhaps you have to go eternally wandering, perhaps in this way you're fulfilling some higher unknown purpose. It's not for nothing that popular wisdom declares we all walk in the eye of God. You're off, then,' went on Lezhnev, seeing that Rudin had picked up his cap, 'you won't be staying the night?'

'I'm off! Good-bye. Thank you . . . I'll come to a bad end.'

'God alone knows that . . . You're definitely going, then?'

'I'm going. Good-bye. Don't remember ill of me.'

'And don't you remember ill of me, either . . . and don't forget what I told you. Good-bye . . .'

The friends embraced. Rudin went out quickly.

Lezhnev spent a long while walking backwards and forwards in his room, then stopped in front of the window, thought, murmured under his breath: 'Poor chap!' and, seating himself at the table, began to write a letter to his wife.

Outside, the wind rose and began to whine with a malevolent whining, striking heavily and spitefully against the ringing panes. The long autumn night set in. Happy is he who sits under a roof on such a night, who has a warm nook to go to . . . And may the good Lord help all homeless wanderers!

In the midday heat of 26 June 1848, in Paris, when the rising of the 'national workshops' was already being suppressed, in one of the narrow streets of the Faubourg St Antoine a battalion of the regular army was taking a barricade. Cannon-fire had already smashed it; those of its defenders who remained alive were abandoning it and thinking only of their own safety when suddenly on the top of it, on the broken body of an overturned omnibus, there appeared a tall man in an old frock-coat with a broad red scarf tied round his waist and a straw hat on his grey dishevelled hair. In one hand he held a red flag, in the other a blunt, curved sword, and he was shouting something in a strained, high-pitched voice, scrambling up the barricade and waving both the flag and the sword. A Vincennes sharpshooter took aim and fired . . . The tall man dropped the flag and fell face forwards like a sack, just as if he was falling at someone's feet ... The bullet had passed through his heart.

'*Tiens!*' said one of the fleeing *insurgés* to another, '*on vient de tuer le Polonais.*'

'*Bigre!*' the other answered and both of them dashed into the cellar of a house with closed shutters and walls pockmarked by bullets and shell-shot.

The *Polonais* was Dmitry Rudin.

Notes

(These notes are taken partly from I. S. Turgenev, *Sochineniya*, T. VI, izd. Akad. Nauk, M.–L., 1963, upon which this translation has been based.)

CHAPTER I

1. *Kammerjunker*. An honorary title bestowed by the Russian Emperor for distinguished service, it was the lowest rank of courtier in the Table of Ranks created by Peter I in 1722. In 1826 the number of such 'gentlemen of the bedchamber' or 'junior chamberlains' was fixed at 36, but later in the nineteenth century the number rose to more than 200.

2. *Zhukovsky*. V. A. Zhukovsky (1783–1852), poet and translator, the friend and protector of Pushkin, Gogol, and many other writers and poets. He is known to have been acquainted with the supposed model for Darya Lasunsky, Alexandra Osipovna Smirnova (née Rosset) (1809–82). Roxolan Mediarovich Ksandryka is supposed to refer to a certain A. S. Strudza (1791–1854), a reactionary official under Alexander I, the author of a number of religious and political works and someone whose claim to expert appreciation of the Russian language – as Pandalevsky claims on his behalf – would be highly suspect.

3. *Thalberg*. Sigismond Thalberg (1812–71), Austrian composer and virtuoso pianist who became very popular in Russia after his successful concert tour in 1839.

CHAPTER II

1. *Rastrelli*. Varfolomey Varfolomeyevich (Francesco Bartolomeo) Rastrelli (1700–1771), Russian architect of Italian extraction, famous as the exponent of Russian baroque, notably in his design of the Winter Palace in St Petersburg.

2. *Dorpat.* Now Tartu, in Estonia; the university was a Swedish foundation dating from 1632.

3. *candidate's degree.* The equivalent of graduating or obtaining what is now a B.A.

4. '*... how she'd done in her own nephew.*' Originally Turgenev included the following lines after this remark:

'Well, sir, I meet Chepuzov, I say to her: "Your nephew, I hear, has died." And she says to me: "That he has, Afrikan Semyonych, that he has; and just imagine," she says, "he comes to me and says 'Auntie, I'm not well, my insides're all in a mess, boo, boo, boo, boo, boo, boo, boo ... oo ... oo ... oo ... boo, boo, boo ... oo ... oo ... oo ... I've got a bad tummy ache, auntie,' he says; I tell him that's nonsense, it's your groin that's hurting! Your groin! Your groin! He insists it's his tummy, and I tell him: It's your groin! Your groin! Your groin! Cure your groin! What d'you think, he didn't listen to me – and he died!" But just take note,' added Pigasov with a look of triumph, 'he actually died of cholera, of cholera, but there was Chepuzov screaming: His groin! His groin!'

'What utter nonsense! What utter nonsense!' Darya Mikhaylovna said over and over again through her laughter.

'I swear to you in all honesty, she was literally screaming: His groin! His groin! Even deafened me, she did, she got so excited. I got involved in a real verbal crossfire. His groin! His groin! She was so worked up she could hardly leave off.'

5. '*... though it's no matter.*' In the line from Griboyedov's *Woe from Wit*, the word used is *incurable*, not *incorrigible*.

CHAPTER III

1. '*I remember a Scandinavian legend.*' What follows is not a 'Scandinavian' legend but the story of the sparrow from the *Historia ecclesiastica gentis anglorum* by the Venerable Bede (673–735). Turgenev may have called it 'Scandinavian' under the influence of Carlyle's interest in Scandinavian mythology.

CHAPTER IV

1. *à la madame Récamier.* Julie Récamier (1777–1849), famous for her 'Grecian' attire as depicted in the painting by David.
2. *Canning.* George Canning (1770–1827), British Foreign Secretary and, briefly, Prime Minister (1827).
3. *quit rent.* Lezhnev's peasants were presumably better off than the majority since, instead of having to perform certain services for their master (i.e. forced labour in the fields, or *barshchina*, as it was called), they paid him a rent in money or in kind (*obrok*).

CHAPTER V

1. *Dumas fils and the like.* The reference is presumably to Alexandre Dumas *fils* (1824–95) who first published in 1847 and did not become famous until the appearance of his *La Dame aux camélias* (1848). Turgenev's chronology would seem to be at fault here: Dumas *fils* could not have been popular in the mid 1840s.
2. *Cambyses.* King of Persia (529–522 B.C.), famous for his invasion of Egypt; Louis XIV, King of France (1643–1715).
3. *Pushkin.* Alexander Pushkin (1799–1837), Russia's most famous poet, author of the novel-in-verse *Eugene Onegin*. Natalya could hardly have known *all* Pushkin's work by heart. Perhaps she may have known some of his political verse, which would account for the innuendo of the three dots.
4. *'Of honour all resplendent speaks . . .'* A quotation from Repetilov's monologue in Griboyedov's *Woe from Wit*, Act IV.
5. *Gentlemen of the Pechorin School . . .* A reference to the hero of Lermontov's novel *A Hero of Our Time* (1841).

CHAPTER VI

1. *Goethe's Faust. Faust*, Part One, was published in 1808; Part Two, from which most likely Rudin read, was not completed until shortly before Goethe's death in 1832. Hoffman (1776–1822),

German novelist and composer. Bettina, Elizabeth Brentano von Arnim (1785–1859), famous for her correspondence with Goethe, published in 1835. Novalis, pseudonym of Friedrich von Harden-burg (1772–1801), representative of German Romanticism.

2. *Tartuffe.* The hero of Molière's comedy (1664–9), an epitome of hypocrisy.

3. '... *one half-mad and most charming poet* ...' The reference is thought to be to V. I. Krasov (1810–55), a talented minor poet, friend of Stankevich and Belinsky, although the quoted lines are not to be found among his works. Turgenev presumably made them up.

4. *Manfred.* A reference to Byron's verse drama (1817).

5. *Paul and Virginia.* A reference to the love-story *Paul et Virginie* (1787) by Bernardin de Saint-Pierre (1737–1814).

CHAPTER VII

1. *La Rochefoucauld.* François La Rochefoucauld (1613–80), author of *Maximes* (1665). In fact, La Rochefoucauld said: 'Confidence in oneself will be the greatest part of one's confidence in others.'

2. '... *on my little fingers.*' This was the only outward sign of being a freemason and, very frequently, all that membership of a Masonic Lodge entailed.

CHAPTER VIII

1. *Aybulat.* The reference is supposed to be to the pseudonym of a little-known poet K. M. Rozen, whose poem 'Two Questions', from which the lines come, was published in 1839.

CHAPTER IX

1. *Lovelace.* The hero of *Clarissa* (1747–8), the novel by Samuel Richardson (1689–1761).

CHAPTER XI

1. *'Blessed is he who in youth was young . . .'* A quotation from Pushkin's *Eugene Onegin*, Chapter VIII, x.
2. *'Whoe'er has felt will feel alarmed . . .'* A quotation from Pushkin's *Eugene Onegin*, Chapter I, xlvi.

CHAPTER XII

1. *Tsarevokokshaisk or in Chukhloma.* Places as remote as Timbuctoo.
2. *The Prisoner of the Caucasus.* A reference to popular prints depicting scenes from Pushkin's Romantic poem (1822).
3. *Georges de Germany.* The hero of a French melodrama by Ducange and Dinaux, *Trente ans, ou la vie d'un joueur* (1827), which was very popular in Russia during the 1830s.

EPILOGUE

1. *Koltsov.* A. V. Koltsov (1809–42), Russian poet famous for folksongs that have been set to music. The lines come from his poem 'The Crossroads' (1840).

MORE ABOUT PENGUINS, PELICANS
AND PUFFINS

For further information about books available from Penguins please write to Dept EP, Penguin Books Ltd, Harmondsworth, Middlesex UB7 0DA.

In the U.S.A.: For a complete list of books available from Penguins in the United States write to Dept DG, Penguin Books, 299 Murray Hill Parkway, East Rutherford, New Jersey 07073.

In Canada: For a complete list of books available from Penguins in Canada write to Penguin Books Canada Limited, 2801 John Street, Markham, Ontario L3R 1B4.

In Australia: For a complete list of books available from Penguins in Australia write to the Marketing Department, Penguin Books Australia Ltd, P.O. Box 257, Ringwood, Victoria 3134.

In New Zealand: For a complete list of books available from Penguins in New Zealand write to the Marketing Department, Penguin Books (N.Z.) Ltd, Private Bag, Takapuna, Auckland 9.

In India: For a complete list of books available from Penguins in India write to Penguin Overseas Ltd, 706 Eros Apartments, 56 Nehru Place, New Delhi 110019.

IVAN TURGENEV

FATHERS AND SONS

Translated by Rosemary Edmonds, with the Romanes Lecture 'Fathers and Children' by Isaiah Berlin

Fathers and Sons is generally agreed to be Turgenev's masterpiece, and its hero, Bazarov, is one of the most remarkable figures in Russian literaure. Turgenev's creation of the first literary nihilist and his demonstration of the failure of communication between generations succeeded in enraging both fathers and sons in the Russia of his time; they also help to explain the appeal of this work to Europeans today. Yet *Fathers and Sons* also contains some of the most moving scenes in the literature of any language.

Also published in Penguin Classics:

ON THE EVE
Translated by Gilbert Gardiner

HOME OF THE GENTRY
Translated by Richard Freeborn

FIRST LOVE
*Translated by Isaiah Berlin
and introduced by V. S. Pritchett*

SPRING TORRENTS
Translated by Leonard Schapiro

SKETCHES FROM A HUNTER'S ALBUM
Translated by Richard Freeborn

DOSTOYEVSKY

CRIME AND PUNISHMENT

When Dostoyevsky began, in 1865, to write the novel that
was to bring him international recognition he was as embarrassed with debts as the hero he created. Raskolnikov, an
impoverished student, decides to murder a stupid and grasp-
ing old woman for gain. After the murder he is unable to
tolerate the growing sense of guilt. This universal theme is
one which had preoccupied the author during his own
imprisonment in Siberia.

THE IDIOT

Perhaps the most appealing of all Dostoyevsky's heroes,
Prince Myshkin, the Idiot, is on one view the pure idealized
Christian and on another the catalyst of a bitter criticism of
the Russian ruling class. This dual vision marks out for the
modern reader *The Idiot* as one of Dostoyevsky's major
novels.

THE BROTHERS KARAMAZOV

Dostoyevsky completed *The Brothers Karamazov*, the culmi-
nation of his work, in 1880 shortly before his death. This
profound story of parricide and fraternal jealousy involves
the questions of anarchism, atheism and the existence of God.

and

THE DEVILS

All volumes translated by David Magarshack

Also published (in translations by Jessie Coulson):

THE GAMBLER/BOBOK/A NASTY STORY
NOTES FROM UNDERGROUND *and* THE DOUBLE

TOLSTOY

All volumes translated by Rosemary Edmonds
WAR AND PEACE

Few would dispute the claim of *War and Peace* to be regarded as the greatest novel in any language. This massive chronicle, to which Tolstoy devoted five whole years shortly after his marriage, portrays Russian family life during and after the Napoleonic war.

ANNA KARENIN

In his masterpiece of humanity Tolstoy depicts the tragedy of a fashionable woman who abandons husband, son and social position for a passionate liaison which finally drives her to suicide. We are also given a true reflection of Tolstoy himself in the character of Levin and his search for the meaning of life.

CHILDHOOD, BOYHOOD, YOUTH

These semi-autobiographical sketches, published in Tolstoy's early twenties, provide an expressive self-portrait in which one may discern the man and the writer he was to become.

THE COSSACKS/IVAN ILYICH/ HAPPY EVER AFTER

The three stories in this volume illustrate different aspects of Tolstoy's knowledge of human nature.

RESURRECTION

Tolstoy's last novel reveals the teeming underworld of Russian society; the rotten heart of his country.

PENGUIN CLASSICS

'Penguin continue to pour out the jewels of the world's classics in translation . . . There are now nearly enough to keep a man happy on a desert island until the boat comes in' – Philip Howard in *The Times*

A selection

Alexander Dumas
THE THREE MUSKETEERS
Translated by Lord Sudley

Cao Xuequin and Gao E
THE STORY OF THE STONE
(also known as *The Dream of the Red Chamber*)
Volume 4: THE DEBT OF TEARS
Translated by John Minford

Anton Chekhov
THE KISS AND OTHER STORIES
Translated by Ronald Wilks

Alexander Pushkin
THE BRONZE HORSEMAN
Translated by D. M. Thomas

Ovid
THE EROTIC POEMS
Translated by Peter Greene

Madame de Sévigné
SELECTED LETTERS
Translated by Leonard Tancock